HIS VIRGIN MATE

INTERSTELLAR BRIDES® PROGRAM: THE VIRGINS - 2

GRACE GOODWIN

Published by KSA Publishers
Goodwin, Grace
Cover design copyright 2020 by Grace Goodwin
Images/Photo Credit: Deposit Photos: diversepixel, aallm

Publisher's Note:
This book was written for an adult audience. The book may contain explicit
sexual content. Sexual activities included in this book are strictly fantasies
intended for adults and any activities or risks taken by fictional characters
within the story are neither endorsed nor encouraged by the author or
publisher.

GET A FREE BOOK!

JOIN MY MAILING LIST TO BE THE FIRST TO KNOW OF NEW RELEASES, FREE BOOKS, SPECIAL PRICES AND OTHER AUTHOR GIVEAWAYS.

http://freescifiromance.com

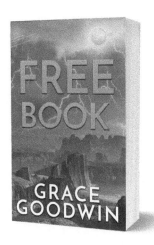

INTERSTELLAR BRIDES® PROGRAM

YOUR mate is out there. Take the test today and discover your perfect match. Are you ready for a sexy alien mate (or two)?

VOLUNTEER NOW!

interstellarbridesprogram.com

1

a lexis Lopez- Interstellar Brides Program Testing Center- Miami

Fingers stroked gently over my cheek. Featherlight and soft. Even so, I felt callouses, and the stark contrast sent a shiver down my spine. I couldn't see the man, but I *knew* him. Felt more than just his caress. I felt his desire, his eagerness for me. How? I had no idea. It made no sense, but I didn't want to think too much. I just wanted to feel.

"Cold?" he asked, his voice a dark rasp.

I shook my head. I was hot. My breasts were heavy and sensitive. Between my legs, my pussy clenched and pulsed with need, with want...with something precious I'd never felt before. Lust.

On my hip, a strange heat spread through me, somehow connecting me to this man, this stranger. I didn't know who he was, but I knew the mark. It burned, sending lightning through my blood and straight to my clit with a powerful jolt I'd never felt before, never dared imagine.

But no. That was wrong. I had a mark like that, but not on my hip. I licked suddenly dry lips, wondering what it would feel like if he touched my birthmark. Mine was on my...

"Don't do that, love." His finger moved to my bottom lip, sliding back and forth. "If you wet your lips like that, I'll dream of you licking my cock."

Heat flared in my core and I whimpered. Memories lingered on the edge of reason, but I couldn't quite reach them. Somehow, I knew this man, knew his scent and his taste. I craved him, and I'd never wanted any man.

Nothing about this made sense, but I didn't want this dream to end. Ever. All my life I'd wondered what the other girls sighed and giggled about. They'd talked of little else for a while now. Me, the odd man out. Or woman, I suppose. I'd never been interested in a man's attentions, never felt lust when I looked at a man, especially one I didn't know. I'd settled on being odd, a cold fish. Broken. But suddenly, with *him?* My body was alive with lust. With want. I could think of little else but tasting him, feeling him. I knew, somehow, in the way one knows things in a dream, that he was going to take me. He was going to fuck me and make me his forever. And I wanted it, so badly, my entire existence narrowed to him. His scent. His voice. The rough calloused fingertip still stroking my lip.

"Do you want to taste my cock again, mate?"

Mate? What? Confusion hindered me for a moment, but this new me, this dream me, wanted him. Now. I gave myself to the moment, eager to have my curiosity assuaged. I'd never been with a man. I wanted to know what it felt like to have him inside me. This man. He was mine. And the picture he painted with his words was exciting.

I knew about a man's cock. I was a virgin, not an idiot,

but I didn't know the nuances of what he'd do to me with it. I didn't know what it would feel like inside me, or what he might taste like on my tongue. Blow jobs were talked about. A lot. In high school, girls even gave them on the school bus. Me? Never. I had no interest in any of the boys I'd gone to school with, let alone their pencil dicks.

But *him?* My mouth watered to taste his cock, to feel the thick, heavy weight of it on my tongue.

His finger slipped away, replaced by his lips. He was kissing me! This wasn't like Bobby Jenkins from tenth grade. We weren't behind the gym. This guy didn't have braces.

No, this wasn't a boy. This was a *man.* With a hand cupping my nape, he angled me as he wanted, his mouth firm and insistent. He put his tongue in my mouth and it was so good. Incredible, licking into me in slow, luscious strokes. This was what it was supposed to feel like? Heat spread through my body like molasses through my veins, thick and slow.

"Has a man ever kissed you before?" he asked, his lips brushing over mine, then along my jaw.

I shook my head in his steady hold.

"What else have you done, mate? Who has touched this soft skin? Kissed you here?" His lips traced my collarbone and I swayed in his arms, longed for his lips to travel lower, to my nipples. Maybe even lower. I'd never had a man's mouth on me before, not down there.

God, I'd never done anything. What a joke I must be to him. "No one. No one else. Ever." I forced the admission past my closing throat and waited for his laughter or raised brow. Who would believe it these days? A twenty-one-year-old working-class girl who was still a virgin. If I admitted it back home, I'd be laughed out of the neighborhood.

I swallowed, then whimpered again when he nuzzled my

ear, lightly nipped the lobe. His hands wandered from the small of my back to cup my ass, his thumb stroking over the sensitive mark on my hip. My legs nearly collapsed as shockwaves of desire made me tremble. I was naked, completely naked in his arms, and his rough clothing brushed against my sensitive skin like sandpaper. My nipples pebbled and I moaned, leaning my head back to give him better access to my neck. I'd never done that before either, but I would give this man who called me mate anything. Everything.

"I never wanted anyone before." Sad, but true. I'd never felt like his. Hot and wet and achy.

"Good," he whispered. "You're mine, and I don't share."

That was just fine with me. Closing my eyes, I reached for him, trying to bury my hands in his hair and pull him closer. But as hard as I tried, I couldn't seem to find a grip. It was like he faded, my hands closing around empty air.

He pulled back and I felt cold. Alone.

"Come back," I pleaded.

"You are a virgin?" he asked. While he no longer touched me, I heard the need in his voice. I'd made him sound that way. Me!

"Yes." I nodded my head and my hair fell over my cheek. I heard tears in my voice, not sad or angry tears, but love and happiness filled this body so full it hurt. Somehow, I knew him, *knew* he was mine. Somehow, I knew he loved me, really, really loved me. The tears were like my heart leaking onto my face.

"Do you want me to be your first?" I could no longer see him, but his voice whispered over me from right behind my ear.

"Yes."

"Will you accept my claim? And claim me as your mate in return? Forever?"

"Yes," I repeated. I didn't know him, but somehow, this body did. I felt like I was someone else, someone magical and powerful, someone not so afraid of being a failure in bed. If he made me feel this good from just a kiss, what would it be like when he touched me in earnest? What would it feel like to have his hard, hot body, his skin, pressed to mine? His cock inside me? His mouth claiming mine as he thrust into me slowly, taking his time, our hands entwined.

Every romantic notion I'd ever had was flooding my mind and I knew he'd give them to me. He was the one. He was going to make me happy. So happy.

"Dream of me." His voice faded to little more than a whisper and I tried to hold on, but the dream slipped away like water through my fingers.

Dream of me.

My eyes opened then and I took in my surroundings, blinking. It took a few moments for my brain to kick back in gear, to realize none of it hadn't been real. The man. The kiss. Nothing.

My cheeks were wet, and I realized I'd actually been crying. Now they fell for a different reason. Loss. I was bereft. Empty. Back to my cold, calm center that so far, nothing had breached. Nothing but *him.*

I was in the Interstellar Brides Processing center. The testing room was small, utilitarian, with a table and chairs, looking more like a drab doctor's exam room than a space-age matching facility. It was the testing unit I sat in that stirred my memory. My wrists were restrained to the metal arms of a chair not much different than the one I sat in at the dentist.

Still, the restraints bothered me. I knew women convicts

could volunteer to be brides. Perhaps the restraints were required since they were prisoners when they arrived. Maybe they tried to break free from here. Maybe, they were just violent or mean and the testing program didn't want to take any chances.

But I wasn't a convict. Me? I hadn't even stolen a pack of gum from the corner store in junior high like my stupid friends. I didn't cheat on tests or lie to my mother. I was boring and sad and pathetic and so lonely I could barely function. The warden had said the cuffs were for my safety. When she strapped me in, I worried about how dangerous the testing would be. But then she walked away from me with a smile and ran her finger over that tablet and I remembered nothing else.

That dream wasn't dangerous. Dangerous to my virginity, maybe. My ovaries were certainly awake now.

I shimmied in the curved seat, but I wasn't going anywhere. It was curved and angled back as if I were going to get a cavity filled, not be matched to an alien mate.

"Are you okay, Alexis?"

Thankfully, the warden had her name on her uniform to help me remember. Egara. She was quite nice, especially considering the Interstellar Brides Program was so streamlined and efficient. Even a tad militaristic. But she'd eased my mind, made me feel good about my decision to be tested. The ads I'd seen on TV promoting the program showed women happily mated to aliens from other planets. The love on their faces—and the obvious well-fucked glow about them—had piqued my interest, but I hadn't done anything about it. Until now. Until I had absolutely nothing left to lose.

Now, I was ready. My dad was dead, my mom had been gone for two years and my Golden Retriever, Rosie, got freaking bone cancer a week after my dad passed and I lost her, too. My best friend since I was eleven, that dog listened to more crying and horrible pop music than any animal ever. But she'd stayed by my side, slept in my bed when I was home, and kept me company at my dad's bedside when no one else was around.

I loved that dog. I loved my parents, too. But they were all gone now. Everything was gone but the big rambling house I couldn't stand to be in. The yard was huge, the house a four-bedroom monster I didn't want to keep. Being in that house, looking at the pictures on the walls, the furniture, the smells...

Being there felt like being in a shrine to my dead parents, and I just couldn't do it anymore. So I sold it, put the money in a trust for my cousin's new baby girl, rented a car and drove to Miami. Three days from Denver. I'd barely slept. Eaten even less.

I felt empty. Totally empty. Until now. Until that dream. And the tears just kept coming, like a silently leaking faucet. That man made me *feel*. He made me want. Hunger. Lust. That girl in the dream was so unlike me. She was full of hope and love, and had joy bubbling in her veins like fizzy candy under her tongue.

I wanted that. I wanted to feel like that.

"Miss Lopez? Can you hear me?"

I blinked at the warden, clearing the cobwebs from my thoughts. Those thoughts were for the past, the tangled, twisted, painful past that I was leaving behind. Today. Right now.

"Yes, I'm all right. That was fast." It seemed like just a minute ago I settled into the chair in my drab hospital-style gown with the Interstellar Brides Program logo printed all over it.

"Yes, it was," she replied. I heard the surprise in her tone and I frowned, felt dread settle in my stomach.

No guy had ever made me feel a tenth of what I'd felt in that dream. I'd never had the hots for a guy on Earth. Ever. I'd gone to the doctor about a year ago to find out if I had a hormonal imbalance or something, but she'd just smiled, looked at my bloodwork and told me everything was perfectly normal. She said there was nothing wrong with my body. I was healthy as could be.

She'd even suggested I visit a counselor of some kind. A therapist. Then she'd started asking me about my papa and uncles and I'd shut her up and gotten the hell out of there.

I didn't have secrets like that in my past. Even if I had, and I had friends who had suffered abuse and rape, they weren't like me. They worked through their past, found a way to be in relationships. They, at least, wanted to try.

Me? No. There was definitely something wrong with me. Hank had called me frigid when I pushed away his advances last year. Of course, he was handsy and smelled of garlic. Robert had said I was a prude, not interested in giving him a BJ after our second date, payment, he'd said, for taking me out to dinner. Twice.

I'd left him sitting in his car in front of my apartment with his dick in his lap. After seeing the bulging, veinous head, I had to wonder why any woman would want to put that in her mouth. Even now, I shuddered at the memory.

Every kiss I'd ever had, from the peck on my cheek from Will Travers in fifth grade to the first French kiss behind the bleachers in tenth, had left me feeling nothing but sloppy, cold and wet.

I didn't fit in. Clearly, men didn't find me appealing and my clit must be broken. I felt nothing when it came to men. I even wondered if I was gay. I'd spent a month after Robert and the cock incident looking at women, studying them, wondering if I might find myself attracted to their bodies. I'd asked a friend of a friend, Meg, who was a lesbian, how to tell if one was actually gay. She'd said if I didn't want to *dive in the bushes,* then I probably wasn't interested in women.

She kissed me once, because I asked her to. And I felt nothing. Nada.

Since the thought of putting my mouth on another woman, *down there,* held about as much appeal as putting my mouth on Robert's cock in the parking lot, I figured I wasn't a lesbian. Which kind of sucked. I didn't care who I might fall in love with, I just wanted to *fall.* I wanted to *feel* desire. I had loved my parents, but that wasn't the same. I loved my dog. I had friends I cared deeply about in high school. Cute memes of kittens and puppies and babies online made my heart lurch. So, my heart worked just fine.

Since I wasn't into women, and no man I'd met made me hot, made me pant like I saw on TV, I finally gave up. I just buckled down and worked. I went to school and studied to be a chef because the only thing I was passionate about was food. The tastes, the textures, the surprises that could roll over my tongue when I combined spices or ingredients in unexpected ways. I'd spent the last three years in school, learning everything I could at the culinary institute downtown.

I excelled in class, but I felt like life was parading in front of me in a twisted and cruel taunt. As the monotony of caring for first one ill parent and then another wore me down, I discovered that going to class made me feel twice as lonely heading home at the end of the day as I did in the morning. The people in my classes were working in real kitchens, earning their place already while I had to squeeze every moment of study I could into my day.

Eventually, I had to stop going to class and take care of my father. We couldn't afford a nurse, or a nursing home. And I couldn't' bear the thought of him wasting away in a place like that while I sautéed mushrooms and made cream sauces for wealthy tourists.

I took care of my father, and every day I thought more and more about the Interstellar Brides Program advertisements. They assured their matches were ninety-nine percent successful. Those were crazy numbers since the divorce rates I'd heard quoted for regular Earth marriages were around fifty percent.

Ninety-nine percent sounded really damn good. And if I didn't have to go on any more dates with guys like Robert, and I was guaranteed a guy that was perfect for me, then I was all for it. What the hell? I had nothing to lose.

Even if that *guy* was an alien.

"Hmm." Warden Egara paced beside me, her dark brown hair up in a bun and her total attention on the tablet in her hand. She didn't look happy anymore. She looked worried.

Maybe I was really, really broken. Maybe their system didn't work on girls like me, stupid, scared virgins who had no idea what to do with a man, let alone an alien.

Oddly, that thought dried the tears immediately. Pain and loneliness I could deal with. Hope hurt a hell of a lot more.

"It didn't work, did it? You couldn't find me a match." I sighed, tried not to let the disappointment make my voice quiver. "I knew it."

"Knew what?" she wondered.

"That I'm broken, that there's something definitely wrong with me when it comes to men."

The warden offered me a sad little smile. Yeah, I was that pitiful. "Oh, no Alexis. I'm sorry. I didn't realize you were worried. I should have spoken sooner. You have been matched."

My heart skipped a beat and my eyes widened. "I have? Really?"

There was someone out there for me? Who was waiting for me right now?

"Really," she repeated, now smiling fully.

"Who?" I knew I sounded breathy and excited, but I couldn't help it. Today, the dream, was the first time I was hot for a guy. Ever. And I had no idea who he was, or *where* he was.

With a swipe of her finger over her controls tablet, the restraints retracted. I sat up, rubbed my wrists, although the hold hadn't been too snug.

"All brides are matched to a planet first, then a mate. For you, and this is quite interesting, your genetic profile matched you to Everis." Her shrewd gaze raked over me. "It seems you have met the special requirements that are very specific to that planet."

"Oh? What kind of requirements?"

She tilted her head to study me. "Let me see your palm."

I didn't know which one, so I rolled my hands over, palms up so she could see both.

She frowned. "Strange."

2

I LOOKED DOWN AT MY HANDS. "WHAT'S STRANGE?"

"All Everians are born with a mark on their palm."

She didn't say more than that, just eyed me. "In order to be matched to Everis, you must have a mark somewhere. Do you have an unusual birthmark anywhere on your body? A large birthmark that runs in your family?"

Holy shit. "Yes." Instinctively, I lifted my arms and wrapped them over my breast to hide the mark there. "Why?"

Her dark gaze followed the movement of my arms, but she smiled. "Long ago, Everian explorers colonized many worlds. Some of their ancestors made it all the way here, to Earth."

"And? What does that have to do with me?"

The warden's face was kind, but her words made my head spin. "Their descendants carry the birthmark you are trying to hide. Your ancestors make you a potential marked mate of an Everian Hunter. Your genetic profile alone would have sent you to Everis. The processing protocols confirmed your psychological compatibility."

"What?" What? Was she saying that *I* was an alien? "I'm from Denver. My family is from Vera Cruz. My *abuela* still lives in Mexico. I'm not an alien. I went to East High School. I was born in Denver."

"Of course you're not an alien, my dear." She whirled and waved her hand in the air to indicate the chair I still sat in and the bank of computers and screens built into the wall. "You're just the descendant of one." She glanced down at her tablet. "According to your genetic profile, you are seventeen percent Everian and eighty-three percent human." She smiled proudly, like a mother bragging about her child's accomplishments in school. "Even after thousands of years, the Everian DNA is very resilient."

"What? If you already knew I was some kind of alien, why did I even go through the test?"

"Your DNA profile placed Everis at the top of your probability matrix. However, the testing you just completed uses many variables to define your wants and needs in a mate based on conscious and subconscious thought. Planets are removed from your options one by one based on these until only one planet remains. At the end of the testing, sexual compatibility is analyzed and ultimately, a recorded mating ceremony is fed to your core brain processing for verification."

I tried to translate her complex wording. "You mean I watched a sex tape from Everis in my mind? Dreamed it?"

She nodded as she sat at the table across from me and

crossed her legs like we were at a tea party or something. "Technically, your body experienced sensual data recorded by the neural processing unit implanted in another bride. But, if you'd like to think of it as a dream, then yes."

"But I didn't dream about sex," I countered, blushing. I could only imagine what a dream with actual sex in it would have been like. A mental porno. "How do you know I'm compatible if I didn't dream about sex?"

"Perhaps you did not dream of intercourse." She lifted a brow and now I felt like she was looking into my soul. "But you did feel desire, did you not? Lust? Hunger? A yearning so fierce your entire body shook with wanting his touch?"

I flushed hotly. All over. I couldn't look her in the eye. God, how did she know?

"You must be a virgin. Correct?" she asked.

I bit my lip and nodded, ashamed to tell her what I was thinking, that I wasn't a virgin by choice, but because I was broken. Then I remembered I was sitting in a gown and that I was naked beneath the soft cotton. I also remembered that she'd probed my deep, inner thoughts.

"Do not be ashamed. On Everis, virginity in a mate is highly honored. Your mate will be pleased, and eager to claim you."

I plucked at the hem of the gown. "But doesn't my mate need to know that I'm...frigid?"

Warden Egara's mouth fell open, snapped shut and opened again. "Clearly the men you've dated were all assholes if you were told that."

I snorted at her word choice. She looked so prim and proper in her uniform and she was talking about asshole guys like we were besties doing tequila shots at my favorite bar. I felt much better.

"I am not a doctor, Miss Lopez."

"Lexi, please."

"Lexi, did it ever occur to you that perhaps you were frigid for other men because they weren't your one true match? Because he wasn't Everian?"

I thought. And thought. Was that true? Could that be true? Had my body been waiting for an alien? Did that seventeen percent of my DNA make me not feel attracted to human men?

Pain knifed through my chest. Ah, there it was again. Hope. Maybe I wasn't broken. Maybe I was an alien girl who just didn't like human guys. The thought made me cringe. What was worse? Being frigid? Or not being human? And what about my parents?

If one of them was like me, no wonder I was an only child. It wasn't like they were chasing me out of the bedroom when I was little. They'd always seemed so kind to one another. But passion? No. They'd been more like best friends.

Suddenly my entire life was twisting and turning in my mind. My mother. She had a mark like mine on her back. She'd had me late in life, been almost forty when she married my papa. Had she been like me and given up on finding passion?

Holy shit. My mother was part alien, too?

Before I could digest that, the warden was talking again.

"Your testing was one of the shortest ever done. That is because you were immediately matched to Everis and, due to your level of sexual experience, they do not wish for you to have any predisposed idea of what will happen sexually with your mate. There is nothing wrong with you. Your match is ninety-nine percent perfect."

She watched me closely and I gave her a small smile.

Predisposed ideas? Like what? Was I supposed to pretend I had no idea what was going on? That I'd never seen porn? Never tried to feel something?

Still, ninety-nine percent perfect sounded really, really good to me.

"Okay." I didn't know what else to say. I was matched, there was a guy out there for me. An almost perfect match. It wasn't as if I could argue with her further. My new mate would find out whether or not I was broken soon enough.

"Okay?" she repeated. I nodded. "Great. For the record, state your name."

I cleared my throat. "Alexis Lopez."

"Are you legally married?"

"No."

"Do you have any biological offspring?" When I eyed her funny, she continued, "I know. A virgin having kids, but I have to ask for the record. You are a special case."

"No. I'm not the Virgin Mary. I don't have any children."

"Do you accept the match that has been given you by the Interstellar Brides Program processing protocol?"

Did I want to leave Earth and go to Everis? To a male who wanted me as pure as the driven snow? Who would revere me for it?

"Yes. I accept."

"Excellent." The warden swiped her finger a few more times on the tablet.

"Thank you, Lexi. By accepting the match, you are no longer a citizen of Earth and are now a matched bride of Everis. As Everis requires unusual protocols, you will not be transported directly. You will transport with two other matched women. I believe one is still being processed. When all of you are done, you can meet. Once Everis has given us the transport coordinates for the Touchstone, you will return here to this room for processing."

She stood, tucked her tablet under her arm.

"If you'll follow me, we'll go check on the others."

———

I FOLLOWED THE WARDEN DOWN A SHORT, BRIGHTLY LIT corridor. The cold tile floor made me wish for some slippers or booties or something. Feminine voices were muffled by a closed door, which the warden opened without knocking.

"Do you have the birthmark, too?"

I heard the question as I walked behind Warden Egara into the room, one hand on the back of my testing gown to keep my butt from being exposed. The small space was an actual conference room with a table and chairs. Two women were huddled together in gowns that matched mine and looked up at me.

"You're here!"

They both stood and came over to me, big smiles on their faces. Their easygoing personalities and bright eyes helped soothe my frazzled nerves. Their excitement was a little startling, but it was reassuring to know they weren't scared of what was happening to us.

"I'm Katie and she's Dani."

"Lexi."

"Did they ask you about the birthmark, too?" Katie asked. She was tall and thin, perfect breasts and curvy hips. Her long brown hair went halfway down her back and was artfully done. Her makeup perfectly framed dark blue eyes that seemed too big in her face. She looked like all the girls in high school who made fun of my curves, but the smile she gave me only felt friendly, not malicious.

I exhaled, not realizing I'd been holding my breath. "It isn't just me then? Who knew we were all aliens?"

They both laughed.

"We're all matched to Everis." Dani went back to her chair, tugging me by the wrist to sit beside her. She was strikingly different than Katie with her gazelle-like looks. Her hair was very blonde and pulled back into a ponytail. There was something graceful about her, as if she were a ballerina. Her body was slim—narrow hips and small breasts —that only added to my perception. She was small and fragile looking, but her gaze was fearless. Katie sat on her other side and I sat beside them, my darker skin, black hair and curves making us all unique. And *we* were part alien? All three of us?

"Are you guys virgins, too?" I asked. I wanted to know if my lack of libido was just me, or if what the warden suggested was true. What if my lack of interest in guys really was caused by alien DNA? When the other two nodded, something tight and ugly began to unravel in my chest. "So, nobody ever rocked your world? You never had the hots for a guy and went for it?"

"Not me." Dani glanced away as Katie blushed.

"Um, no. Virgins, virgins *everywhere.*" Katie tucked her long brown hair back behind her ear. "Do you think this is a little weird? Three virgins with strange birthmarks being sent to an alien world? I feel like a virgin sacrifice. Like they're going to line us up and march us into a volcano or something." Her laugh was brittle, and not completely in jest.

"My match was ninety-nine percent," I admitted, oddly proud of that. "I might be a sacrifice, but the guy is supposedly all mine."

Dani smiled, rubbed her hands together. "God, I'm so

nervous! My match was that high, too, which means...there's a guy on the planet who will actually think I'm hot!"

I thought she was hot and I didn't even like women. I had to wonder about the men she'd been around for her to have such a low opinion of herself, and then I realized I was just like her. We looked nothing alike but seemed to have had the same problems with men in the past. And with our own self-esteem issues.

Katie pursed her lips. "My match was only ninety-eight percent."

Dani rolled her eyes. "Where are you guys from?"

"Denver, Colorado," I said.

"I'm from Wooster, Ohio," Katie added.

"Gainesville, Florida." Dani grinned and I could easily imagine her in a bikini and sunglasses on the beach. "And we're all going to Everis. Together. You know what this makes us? BFFs."

I looked at the other two women, recognized kindred spirits. We were very similar, perhaps not personality-wise, but we were all matched to Everians. We were all virgins and we were going to be transported together. We would be the only friends from home, all each other had once we got to Everis. We might have been from different parts of the US, but we were all from Earth. I'd say that made us BFFs.

"Let's make a pact," Katie said.

Dani wiggled in her chair. "Yes! We share everything. No holding back. Even embarrassing things like sex and orgasms and toys. Whatever they do to us, we have to talk. Okay? We're all each other has, right?"

"Besides each of us having a hot, alien hunk who wants to take our virginity?" I asked, an excited grin on my face. The thought of feeling the kind of desire I'd just experienced in that processing dream made my heart skip a beat.

"Those are guys. No offense, but they don't count. Not for this. Us girls have to stick together," countered Dani.

"Like the three musketeers," Katie added.

"All right," I said. "I agree, but I'm not drawing blood or spitting in my palm."

Katie cringed. "Yeah, no. Gross. Yes, to the pact. We spill. And I mean details."

"Details," Dani repeated.

When Warden Egara lifted her head from her tablet and said it was time, we grabbed each other's hands. "Details," I added.

We had to part in the hallway, each of us going back to a separate testing room for our final processing.

"Will it hurt?" Katie asked Warden Egara.

The warden shook her head. "Not at all. You'll be processed and transported. Before you know it, the three of you will be together at the Touchstone gathering on Everis. There, you will meet your mates. Good luck, ladies."

I looked to Katie and Dani. Gave them each a small smile. This was it.

Katie, who seemed to be the most adventurous, gave a little wave of her fingers and dashed into her testing room, her bare butt the last we saw of her. Dani rolled her eyes and went next. I stood in the quiet hallway with Warden Egara.

"Would you go, if you were me?" I asked her. I figured Katie and Dani were talking up going to Everis because of nerves. Pep talk. I didn't blame them. But Warden Egara was more impartial.

"I did. I was mated to a Coalition warrior." She turned and walked into the testing room and I followed, curious about her answer.

"You were? On Everis?" I asked, sitting down once again in the testing chair.

She shook her head, but looked down at her tablet. Flicked her finger once, twice. The restraints returned about my wrists.

"No. Prillon."

She'd been sent to Prillon Prime? I'd heard of the planet, of the big—no, huge—warriors. The way they claimed their mate with a second male. She'd had *two* mates? Yet she was here, on Earth? "You had two mates?"

"Yes."

She didn't offer details, but I couldn't seem to stop myself from pushing. I knew my mother would be rolling in her grave at my lack of manners, but I couldn't stop the words from flowing out of my mouth. "What happened? Why are you here?"

"My mates died, Lexi," she sighed. "I was a special case, a long time ago. Would I go again? Would I be you if I were ten years younger?"

I nodded. I watched her face, looked at her eyes for any deception.

"Absolutely."

I saw sadness but no regret and that made me feel better.

"Ready?" she asked.

"Yes." I took a deep breath, let it out.

She pressed a button and the wall behind my head opened. I couldn't see very well, but a soft blue glow came from it. As if on a Disney World ride, the chair tilted back, slid through the wall, which seemed to be a small space, just right for my testing chair. A robotic arm with a needle came silently toward me. I winced when it pierced my skin.

"Do not be afraid. You will be given an NPU. The Neural Processing Unit will be placed just behind your ear and will allow you to speak and understand Coalition languages. You will be processed and transported to Everis."

The chair lowered into a warm bath, the blue glow even brighter. All of my fears melted away like a snowball in the sun. I was going to Everis to meet my matched mate and I was finally going to—

"Your processing will begin in three... two... one."

3

*S*enior Hunter Von, Planet Everis

I WAS EAGER TO RETURN TO BED. TO SLEEP AND DREAM. OF her. She was close, so close my body operated in a nearly constant state of arousal. In the weeks since my return from fighting the Hive in deep space, I'd wanted nothing but peace, the quiet of the wind in the trees and the water pouring over stones in the river. Quiet and solitude.

I'd been rewarded with neither. The high mountain home my battalion had been *gifted* after our return from the war was more than large enough for the group of soldiers who now occupied its cold stone walls and fortifications. We were tasked with governing the region, settling disputes and meting out punishment for those who broke our laws. We were Hunters now, protectors of the weak, keepers of the peace, and justice for any criminal foolish enough to break Everian law.

Things had been busy since our assignment to Feris 5. We

were fifty strong, with a small army of servants and underlings to do our bidding. But the Touchstone, the fortress where unclaimed mates were transported and housed, was in the center of my territory, and every few weeks, when a new batch of potential mates arrived, I brought at least twenty men down from the mountain to keep the peace.

Marked mates were precious and the brides that were transported to the Touchstone arrived ready to be claimed. Alone. Protected only by protocol and the honor of the men vying for their hands.

But my bed was empty. Had been for years, but each night since I'd returned to Everis and submitted to the testing, the void grew inside me. I was used to being alone. I was damn good at it. A fact that hadn't bothered me until last night when I had the first dream.

A dream of her. My mate. My marked mate.

My only thought, the only possibility was that she transported here from another world. Yesterday, when my mark came awake. Tingled, heated. She was one of the matched mates from another planet. There was no other explanation.

I'd thought since my mark wasn't on my palm that it meant I was defective, that there was no match. No one for me. But it had heated, just like I'd heard from every other Everian who'd come in contact with their marked mate. Yes, it was in a remarkably unusual place, but it worked!

She was at the Touchstone. The dreams proved it. I didn't know her name, but her mind touched mine. I would find her. Seduce her. There would be no mercy in me, not when it came to this. Gods, I'd longed for a mate for years. Fighting the Hive was brutal, and the idea of finding the perfect female, the *one*, had kept me going. Less than one in a hundred Everian men found their marked mates. Most settled into a comfortable life with a comfortable bride. Not all Everian males felt the fire of their marks come to life. But I'd clung to hope. Had used the slim possibility as reason to stay alive so I would have the chance to find her. To make her mine.

And now the chance was here. *She* was here on Everis. At the Touchstone.

I would only have thirty days to convince her to agree to my claim. She might be my marked mate, but there was no law nor protocol to prevent her from choosing another man as her mate in that time. Nothing to guarantee she would choose me.

Nothing but my mouth on her pussy making her scream, my cock filling her up. I would have to take her body in all three ways to claim her. I would make her writhe with pleasure, bury her in my scent and my touch until she could think of no other, want no other.

My cock grew hard and I shifted on the bench where I sat next to my fellow Hunter, Bryn.

Normally, Bryn never shut his mouth, always laughing or tormenting one of us. But he sat beside me, strangely silent as we finished our meal of meat and vegetables. Since returning home, we feasted on *breet* from the north and roasted bird from our native lands. The S-Gen units on the Coalition battleships had provided thousands of options for food, but with so many member planets, programming every delicacy from every world was unreasonable. The engineers in charge of the S-Gen units analyzed the nutritional benefits of common offerings on each world and made sure everyone had enough to keep them healthy. One or two treats was all we'd been allowed. Now, we were home, and my men and I had kept the kitchens busy trying to bring back the simple pleasures of our pasts.

"When do we leave for the Touchstone?" Bryn asked, swirling his dark ale in his glass.

"First light." We weren't due there until late in the day, when the official mating presentations would begin, but I could wait no longer. She was there. My mate. I could not risk delaying one moment more. Duty held us here through the night, but tomorrow we would ride. Not that I would waste the darkness, not now that my mind had found hers. I could not wait to return to my chambers, eager for the next dream I might share with my mate.

Bryn nodded and took the remains of his meal to the recycling unit along the wall. Without speaking to another soul, he exited the dining hall and disappeared.

That conversation was over. I frowned at my friend's odd mood.

Not that I minded. I had a sleeping draught waiting for me in my bedchamber so I could slip easily into slumber. I would hunt her tonight, in my dreams. I would learn her name. Perhaps even see her face.

Conversation flowed around me as Hunters and the other residents of the fortress came and went, eating, laughing, living.

I'd forgotten how to do that. Live. I'd spent too long with the Hive, seeing destruction and chaos. I hoped my mate could snap me out of the darkness that surrounded my heart. Four years of battle. It didn't sound like much, but I seemed slow to adapt to the more relaxed pace of civilian life. Would I ever be able to hear a shout without looking for danger? The crack of a broken twig without looking for enemies? The whir of the fans haunting me like the steady hum of the battleship's air system?

"Hunter Von, sir. I have several new incident reports. We need to dispatch Hunters before we leave for the Touchstone." A junior Hunter spoke from across the table and I nodded to let him know I'd heard. Sleep would wait. My mate would wait, although I put duty before my marked mate for the last time.

Tomorrow, she would be mine.

"I'll be there in a moment."

He spun on his heel and walked away, toward the command room. There we would go over the latest batch of assignments, from requests for assistance to investigating crimes, and I would put men to each task.

The fortress guards were the elite Hunters, protectors. It was important work entrusted to a rare few Everian males. We were the strongest, the fastest, the most skilled Hunters. Most were trained soldiers who had served in the Coalition Fleet and assigned to fortresses around the planet. We were vital to maintaining peace and stability on Everis. I took the role as a privilege I'd earned from the years fighting the Hive. I didn't take it lightly. The role was crucial to the stability and safety of our people.

I knew this. But for the first time, being needed by my people wasn't enough.

And damn my weak heart for wanting more. But I did. I wanted what I saw, heard, smelled, felt in my dream.

Eager to return to my quarters, I went to the command center and made quick work of assigning men to their tasks. While a strong group would remain to protect the fortress, I'd take my strongest and most loyal Hunters with me to the Touchstone tomorrow morning.

Tonight I would dream.

Done with my duties, I made my way to my private quarters and pulled the sleeping draught I'd bought earlier from the drawer next to my bed. I drank it all down and lay back, eager to see her again. To touch her. Even if it was only a dream. Tomorrow, it would be real.

———

Von, Dreamscape

HER LONG BLACK HAIR FANNED OUT ON THE WHITE BED sheets, offering a stark contrast in the moonlight. Sheer white curtains swayed near the open window at the slight breeze. The bedroom was large, with a sofa and table with two chairs for resting, reading, or fucking. Suddenly, I wanted to bend her over that table and fuck her until she begged for release. Then I would position her on the table's edge so the hard surface struck her clit with each thrust of my cock. The table would rock as I took her, as I made her scream her release. But that rough need would have to wait.

I would take her in the sacred order of the three, one at a time. See her surprise as I awakened her body, her mind, to passion. To claim each of her holes for my own. First, it would be her mouth, opening wide to take me deep, to swallow my seed. Then it would be her ass. That hole would be tight, and the sweet feel of her submission as I took her in this most intimate of ways would only tighten our bond as I made her scream and writhe with pleasure. Lastly, I'd take her pussy, feel her inner walls ripple and grip my cock. I'd watch her eyes blur with arousal, feel her juices coat my cock. I'd fill her then, coat her womb with my seed and claim her officially—and permanently—as mine.

Yes.

The large, central bed draped in white. The recessed

lighting provided just enough illumination for me to study my mate's beautiful face as she slept. She was on her side, her arms bent and her hands tucked beneath her chin in a pose both innocent and enticing, for her arms pressed her lush breasts together and offered a tantalizing bit of cleavage. I recognized her room as one of the suites assigned to new brides at the Touchstone center and I felt some small relief.

She would be safe there, protected, until tomorrow when I could find her. As long as she didn't choose another.

My cock rose to attention at the challenge and I longed to join her in that bed, to run my fingers through the shining mass of her black hair and hold her head in place for my kiss as I introduced her to pleasure. She was mine. No other would touched her. None who wished to live. All I needed to do was convince her that I was her marked mate, her destiny. Perfect for her.

I stepped to the edge of the bed and lay down beside her. I imagined the scent of fresh spring flowers and warm honey drifted from her flesh. But this was just a dream. My mind would fill in the blanks, convince me that I touched her, held her, tasted her, but it would all be a lie, a trick of my imagination.

Everything physical would be an illusion.

But her words would be real. As would mine.

Lying on my side, I reached over and traced her full lower lip with my thumb. So fucking soft. I couldn't wait to have that innocent mouth open around my cock.

I traced her curves, from shoulder to hip. Placing my hand on the curve of her waist, I squeezed gently to make her aware of my presence. This remarkable female was mine. My one true mate in the universe. Our minds touched, as only marked mates' could, and I wanted to explore everything about her. What made her smile? What made her angry? I needed to know the taste of the sweet honey that flowed from her pussy, the flavor of her skin. What sounds would she make as I fucked her? Where did she like to be touched?

Her eyes fluttered, then opened wide, her gasp sweet as her heartbeat raced beneath her ribs.

"You came back." Her sexy whisper made my cock ache and my hand seemed to have a mind of its own, tracing her curves from shoulder to hip and back. Over and over. I made sure to brush the side of her breast where I knew her mark must be hiding beneath the cream-colored nightgown. The shimmering fabric clung to every curve. It was beautiful, but I longed to rip it from her body. I needed to see her. Feel her. Claim her.

"Of course I returned. You're mine."

She shivered, but didn't look away. "This is just a dream. You're not real."

Holding her gaze, I lowered my hand to her breast, cupped the soft weight. Gently squeezed the hardened pebble in a tender reprimand. "I am very real."

4

 on

REACHING AROUND HER SLIGHT FRAME, I PULLED HER TOWARD me until her hips met mine. Her gasp assured me she felt what I wanted her to feel, needed her to feel, my hard cock ready and eager to claim her. Her eyelids lowered slowly, her body melting into me as her eyes darkened with passion.

Gods, she was perfect. So innocent, yet so sensual. She had admitted to me last night, in our first dream meeting, that she was virgin, unclaimed. Waking her to her body's passionate nature was going to be a true pleasure. I couldn't wait to claim her in the traditional way, mouth, then ass, and finally, when she accepted my claim, I would fill her sweet pussy with my cum and fill her womb with my child. I wanted her heavy and full with my seed, her body ripe and sensitive. I had longed for, hoped for a mate and children, but never considered I'd be lucky enough to have this happen to me. For so many years I'd been focused on duty and honor, on survival. But now? Seeing her dark eyes and shining black hair, I wanted her. I wanted everything.

"Look at me." I tested her then, needing to know her true nature. Would she welcome the commanding tone of my voice? Or defy me?

She gasped, biting her lip and her hips jerked against mine. But her eyes opened, and her dark gaze held mine. What I saw there nearly made me come. Desire. Trust. Need.

My little mate was as affected as I. Thank the gods.

I knew, if I could reach between her legs and feel her pussy, she'd be wet with welcome. She longed for my dominance, my need to command. Knowing she would surrender so sweetly made me fight back a growl.

"Tell me your name, little one."

She shook her head, denying me this one simple thing. Leaning forward, I pulled her lips into my mouth, nibbling, kissing, then biting gently in reprimand. "I am Von. Tell me your name."

This wasn't real. Gods, I knew it wasn't real, but once I tasted her I couldn't stop. I kissed my way from her lips to her chin, her neck. Lower. She arched her back, her hips pressed to mine as she angled her head to the side in welcome, giving me better access.

"Von." My name was a breathy sigh from her lips and my entire body reacted like she'd just stroked my cock.

I kissed her neck, licking and sucking and tasting. Working my way to her ear, I asked again, "What's your name?"

Her silence both aroused and enticed me. I did not want a pliant, biddable mate. I wanted a woman with fire, a mate who would be fierce and protective of her children. One who would scratch and claw at the world and yet submit so sweetly in bed.

Rolling her beneath me, I took her mouth. I kissed her. Claimed her. Rubbing my cock in the vee of her legs, our clothing and her innocent mind kept me from filling her with my cock. I rubbed my hard length against her core, and her mind allowed the contact, not completely overwhelmed or shocked.

When I lowered my hand to her hip, reaching for the hem of her gown so I could sink my fingers into her hot, wet pussy, I met resistance, an invisible barrier I could not pass.

Inwardly, I groaned. I could not touch her. Not yet. I could not take her farther in a dream than she knew in reality. And no other man had ever touched her sweet center, ever tasted her wet heat or heard her cry out with pleasure. The thought turned me nearly feral, the protective instincts of the Hunter I was rising like the tides to swallow me whole.

This woman was mine. I had thought to act honorably, to give her a choice. But now, seeing her, tasting her, touching her mind, I knew I would move the heavens themselves to keep her. Nothing would stop me from seducing her, from earning her love.

Her skin was softer than a newborn babe's. Her sighs music to my warrior's heart. She wasn't fighting me, she was simply innocent, her mind unable to fabricate lies of passion.

I kissed her again, until her body trembled with need, the air racing in and out of her lungs in uncontrolled bursts.

"Your name, mate?"

"I'm not your mate."

"By the Divine, you are mine. My marked mate." I grabbed her hands and held them above her head, pinning her as I lowered my mouth to the side of her right breast. Her mark would be there. I knew this for a fact as mine was in the same location on the side of my ribs. She was mine. I nuzzled the swell of her breast with my nose, my mouth, my chin, rubbing two days of stubble over her sensitive flesh before kissing and biting through her silken gown. "You have a birthmark, mate. Right here."

She gasped and fought me, but I held her hands in place and she quickly melted, her head thrashing side to side on the pillow.

I kissed that mark, pulled her gown away with my teeth so I could kiss her bare breast. The moment my lips made contact with her naked skin, she moaned. A firestorm of need arced between us as I kissed and suckled her birthmark, the sacred and magical mark that linked us. That made her mine. Proof. I saw it. Felt it.

"I'm coming for you, mate. Wait for me. Do not choose another."

I moved to suck her nipple into my mouth and her hips bucked, her voice barely more than a whisper. "Officiate Treva said there would be eighty males to choose from tomorrow. She said I may choose any man I want."

Flicking my tongue over her nipple until she cried out, I lifted my head at last and kissed her again before answering. "Yes. By law, you may choose any man at the Touchstone. But we both know you won't."

"Why not?"

"Because they won't give you what you need."

Her pulse raced and I lowered my head to kiss her at the base of her throat.

"What do I need?"

"My hand twisted in your hair as I fuck that sweet mouth. My long, hard tongue working your clit, filling your virgin pussy until you wrap your legs around my shoulders and demand I never stop. Until I claim all that is mine. Until you claim me in return."

She was panting now, but there was more. So much more.

I tilted my hips, rubbing her clit with my hard length through our clothes as she whimpered beneath me. I lowered my head so my warm lips would brush her ear as I finished.

"You need me to stretch your ass, take you hard and fast as I fill your pussy with my fingers, making you come again. And again. You need my cock buried balls deep in your pussy, fucking you bare, filling you with my seed over and over as you scream, begging for release."

"Oh my god."

She bucked beneath me, her eyes clouded with mindless lust. For me.

It was time to go. I wanted more, but could not give it to her. I'd done enough, made her as eager and hot as I was. She was aroused by me. Desired me. She might see other males, but I would be the one she longed for. I'd just ensured that.

"You're mine, mate. Wait for me. I will find you."

————

Alexis, Planet Everis, The Touchstone

"As you know, today is the meeting of males and mates here at the Touchstone." The woman we knew as Officiate Treva stood in front of us, the group of twelve women who had been matched through the Brides Program and transported to Everis.

The female looked completely human, but she moved with an almost beautiful efficiency that made me watch her more closely than I normally would. All of the Everians I'd met looked human, but there was something about them, something that screamed *more*. Officiate Treva looked like she was a decade older than Katie, Dani and myself and had a

37

confident bearing the rest of us lacked. Her hair was a dark auburn and hung in a smooth fall to the tops of her shoulders. Her eyes were a warm amber, the color of whiskey and she was the same height as Katie, just above average on Earth. Her uniform was dark navy blue, the marks of her rank on her arm and color in bright silver. I did not know the politics or rankings of people here, but she and the other Officiates were high in the pecking order. I hadn't seen a single Everian argue with her, man or woman. Her bearing and confidence made me feel even more unsure, like a child trying to play in the grown-ups' sandbox. The way Katie and Dani were fidgeting, they must be feeling the same.

We were on a new world, awaiting a roomful of males. I imagined twelve innocent little lambs about to be sniffed and assessed by a roomful of wolves. None of us were Everian, we'd never been to the planet before and knew next to nothing about being mated.

Officiate Treva, however, had shared that she had been tested and matched after her service fighting the Hive was complete. She looked happy. In her Everian uniform she looked crisp and curt, however she was quite relaxed. If she'd had some stranger in a dream show up two nights in a row and tell her all the dark and dirty things he wanted to do to her, maybe she wouldn't look so cool and in control. But, no. If the Officiate was mated, her man wouldn't talk or tease, he'd just *do* it all.

I shifted on my seat at the thought. Von. That was his name. And he said the naughtiest things to me. For once in my life, I wasn't offended by a man's horny rambling. This time, I wanted to hear more. No, this time I wanted to *do* everything.

I'd seen other Everian soldiers—was that what they were called?—walking about, serving as guards and protectors for us, but they had all been overly serious. Like the Secret Service guarding the president. Always on duty, watchful. No one said we were in danger from anything other than overeager Everian males. Maybe they just didn't tell us everything. Or maybe, we were a lot more valuable here than I thought.

Were we Interstellar Brides really wanted that badly? I glanced at Katie, who was biting her lip. We'd transported to Everis together, waking up on beds near one another in the medical unit. Naked and covered only in a sheet, the doctors had waved odd wands over us, performing weird tests to make sure we came through in one piece. Once satisfied, they handed out pretty flowing gowns for us to wear and we were all dressed and shown to our suites. There were four suites occupied at the moment. Three brides per apartment. Katie, Dani and I had asked to be put together, in honor of our pact, so now the three of us shared. That had been two days ago.

Since then, the three of us had become closer, true BFFs, going everywhere together, learning everything about each other's lives on Earth. We weren't able to leave the building, but we were free to roam about. The place was huge, reminding me of a mountain lodge with guest suites, conference rooms and full service, five-star restaurants. It had been amazing. Just us girls—and the guards who never actually spoke to us. Although one of them, a big, handsome man in one of the blue uniforms, had been watching me constantly. He was obviously well-respected, one of the officers or whatever, but he wasn't the man I wanted.

He wasn't Von.

None of the eighty potential mates had arrived until this morning. Once the other men started to show up, we'd figured out that the dark navy uniforms were the Everian version of officers while the brown uniforms were worn by everyone else. They were all military like, with protocols and ranks. The complete control of the Officiates, the sense of order helped me fight off my nerves.

Over the last few hours, I'd looked for those blue uniforms, glad to see them ever watchful and somewhere close. I'd never been stared at so much in my life. Ogled. Katie and Dani agreed that we felt like fresh meat. Most just nodded in passing, returned a smile if it was offered. None pushed or tried to talk to us. Apparently, that was not yet allowed.

But that one man, the blond in blue, stared a lot. And not at all three of us, but at me. At first, I'd been nervous. But now, I wasn't sure what to do. He wasn't hiding his interest, or pretending indifference. No, he wasn't even pretending to be polite. He *stared* like he could take off my clothes with just his eyes. Like he knew something about me that I did not.

And unlike the way Von made me feel in my dream, this man made my skin go cold and my hands shake. And not in a good way. He was powerful. Big. Strong. And he looked at me like I was his prey.

5

*L*exi

HE WAS HANDSOME ENOUGH. PALE HAIR, EQUALLY LIGHT EYES, strong jaw, commanding presence. I was flattered, at first, because it was rare that I made any guy look twice. This one? He looked more than that. His attention became a little disconcerting because his gaze was dark, almost intimidating. I felt no warmth in it. He wasn't the one I shared dreams with. I knew it deep down. I should feel flattered he paid me any attention, but I didn't like it. He made me unsettled. My BFFs, too, for every time he came near us, we hustled the other way.

We were *all* unsettled. All twelve of us. We could talk about what was happening until we were blue in the face, but until the official launch of the events, our first actual meeting with the men, we could only guess how everything worked.

Fortunately, Officiate Treva was giving us something like

an orientation first. Dani gave me a look. I knew what she was thinking. *Why didn't she do this two days ago?*

It hadn't just been the unknown that had worried us, but the sleeplessness. The first night, I'd tossed and turned, riddled with the same dream over and over again, like a really hot broken record. A man in bed beside me, asking me questions, whispering to me, kissing me. *Touching* me. I didn't say anything to the others about it because I'd thought it had just been me, remembering the testing dream back on Earth.

But when we all woke up after a second night of restless sleep, I knew I wasn't the only one who'd been dreaming. Not just one night, but two. We were all edgy over breakfast, quiet. If Katie and Dani were like me, they were thinking about the man in their dreams, what he'd done and most especially, how they'd felt.

God, I'd gotten hotter in a dream than with any real man on Earth. If he'd kept going, I'd have let him. A stranger. The scary and exhilarating part was, I'd have come for him, too. No longer wondering if I was simply asexual, I shuddered under the slightest touch of his fingers. His kiss made my entire body burn. I'd never felt anything like it and I wanted more.

But he'd stopped. Not touching me. Not *taking* me, filling me with his cock. I couldn't even get laid in a dream. Which seemed rather pathetic.

"You all know you were matched to Everis." The Officiate's stern voice brought me back to the real world. "What you may not know is that six thousand years ago, explorers from Everis scattered across the galaxy to colonize new worlds. Earth was one of those worlds."

I nodded. I'd already heard this story from Warden Egara. Treva continued.

42

"You have all been told that you are descendants of those colonists, survivors from our world who mated with humans. What you may not know is the significance of the mark you all bear and how it might help you find your one true mate."

"What?" Katie squirmed and I crossed my arms over my breasts in defense. The floor-length gowns we all wore were beautiful but thin. And we were naked beneath the bright display of color, for we each chose our own.

Treva nodded. "The legends say that long ago, an Everian Hunter so pleased the Divine with his honor and bravery that he was granted a gift, a perfect mate. This Hunter, the very first Hunter of Everis, was granted many special skills. Enhanced speed and strength. An unfailing instinct for the hunt. A strong mind and an iron will. This Hunter had survived a mighty battle and carried the marks of his struggle on his body.

"The Divine saw this and promised the Hunter that a perfect mate had been created for him. Their minds would be as one. Their bodies would unite in perfect harmony. He would find solace and peace in her arms unlike any other." Officiate Treva paced before us like we were soldiers and she was our drill sergeant, but not one of us moved or dared ask a question. I felt like I was in preschool being told a fairy tale.

"The Divine promised the Hunter would know his mate by a special mark placed on her palm by the Divine and loving goddess herself, a mark that matched his exactly, a mark that would feel as if on fire when his mate was near."

"Holy shit." Dani's whispered words didn't carry far, but I heard them and shared the sentiment, although I remembered Warden Egara finding it strange my mark was elsewhere on my body. I wasn't going to worry about it. It heated and tingled now as if it just woke up. I immediately

43

thought of Von, of his mouth on my breast. Was that truly how he'd known about the mark there? Did he really have one in the exact same place? Did it heat and ache and burn, as mine did?

"Are you saying that an Everian male with a mark just like mine is my true mate?" Dani asked.

I leaned forward, eager to hear this answer. It was completely unbelievable, even though Von had murmured the exact thing to me the night before.

"Yes, Dani. And no."

I blinked, confused. "Then what's the point of this story? I don't understand."

Treva stopped pacing and faced us with her hands locked behind her back, her face more serious than I'd ever seen her. "The legend of the marked mate is true, but a marked match is rare. Fewer than one in a hundred find their marked mate. First, you must trigger a psychic connection that causes dream sharing. After that, your Hunter must come to you. He must hunt you to prove his worth, find you, no matter where you are on this world. It is a rare and beautiful gift to have a marked mate."

"What if he doesn't find us?" Dani asked. "Or what if they don't want you, after they meet you? Or dream you? Or whatever?"

Treva looked doubtful, but she shrugged. "It is extremely unlikely any of you will have a marked mate on Everis. If you do meet your marked mate, you will know. Your mark will awaken, become warm, hot even. And tingle."

Katie looked at me and nodded as she rubbed her palm. Dani tilted her hand so her palm was up and stared at it. She hadn't mentioned it heating up, but she did look at the mark there with an odd look, something like surprise.

"You must dream of him, you must establish a link before

he can find you. However, if you do have a marked mate, and he is here, in this building, you are not required to choose him. You are free to choose any male at this gathering. Any male here will be thrilled to be chosen, and will accept you as a mate whether your marks heat or not."

So, there was some kind of magical, mystical connection between marked mates, but almost no one on this planet could find their one perfect love.

Sounded like online dating websites. Lots of promises, not a lot of results.

My *mark* had been there my whole life. I'd thought it a birthmark. Since it was on the side of my breast, no one saw it but me. But soon enough...my mate would surely see it and a whole lot more. Von knew exactly where it was, had kissed it, and the heat that had pulsed through my body at the contact had my nipples hardening, my pussy all but dripping even now. Just as he'd said.

Now that I was here, and now that I'd had two nights of dreams, I was excited. And completely nervous. And horny as hell. Yes, me. The curvy, short, ice princess was horny because a guy had said *Wait for me.*

"So, now that you know the history of our Hunters and their destined brides..." Treva took a moment to glance at each of us. "Anyone have a tough time sleeping?"

One of the other girl's mouth fell open, probably thinking Officiate Treva must have ESP. Clearly, the girl hadn't talked with her roommates about the dreams she'd had. A few others nodded. Two looked completely confused.

Dani, Katie and I shared a quick glance. We all knew the score. We'd all been dreaming.

"Why didn't the dreams happen before now?" Dani wondered. She seemed to have lots of questions and wasn't afraid to ask. "If I have a mate, why didn't I dream share with him two years ago?"

Treva smiled like a teacher pleased with her student. "Good question. The answer is simple. Area of proximity. Dream sharing only occurs when your marks are within a certain distance of each other. Earth is seven light years away. That's too great a distance for the connection to be made. So when you arrived here, you entered the area of proximity to your mate and the dreams began. It sounds a little farfetched, but your mark *woke up* after you arrived if your mate was close enough."

"I didn't dream share," a petite blonde woman said, worry creasing her brow. The girl beside her also nodded.

Officiate Treva held up her hand. "That is normal, dear. As I said, a marked mating is extremely rare. You may choose any male here, or you can choose to wait. You are welcome to live here, cared for and protected at the Touchstone, for as long as you like. Perhaps your mate is not nearby. Perhaps he is on a battleship fighting the Hive, or on the other side of the world."

"Great. Now I'll never find him." The girl looked upset, and I didn't blame her. Knowing I'd already shared my dreams with Von took away my fear in that regard.

Treva walked to the girl and placed her hand on the young bride's shoulder. "The bi-monthly Touchstone events are well known on Everis, especially now since the discovery and arrival of marked female descendants from Earth. For those males who have yet to find their mate on Everis, you give them hope. They will come, I promise you. And if you do not have a marked mate, there are any number of Hunters here who would do anything to make you happy. You can have a very successful mating, even if the man you choose is not your marked mate."

"What if I don't like my mate?" Katie was the Debbie Downer of the three of us, but I was glad she asked the question. While I seemed to find my mate *very* pleasing in the dreams we shared and I was eager to meet him in real life, that didn't mean I'd really like him enough to keep him forever. An orgasm was one thing. Forever was another. What if he was a jerk? Bossy? Arrogant? Cruel?

"There is a connection between an Everian male and female. Don't forget, while you were born and raised as a human, your mark proves that you are also part Everian. The bond is strongest between Everians. If you do not like your mate, or do not find him, then you may choose any Everian male you wish. Per Interstellar Brides processing protocols, you were matched to the planet, not a specific mate. The choice is yours, ladies. Always."

"But the mark does that. Match us to our true mate," Dani countered.

"Correct. Your marked mate is the *strongest* match. It does not mean it is the only one for you. That is why you have thirty days to accept or reject a Hunter's claim. We follow Coalition law. You will be claimed. Once a Hunter has stated his intention, he has thirty days to win your consent. If you accept his claim, he will be your mate for life. If you do not, you will remain here, at the Touchstone, and go through the claiming process again."

It wasn't exactly speed dating, but it wasn't forever either. A month. And I could say no. That eased some of the tension from my jaw and shoulders and I relaxed. Thirty days. I could do thirty days.

Several of the other women's shoulders dropped as well and I grinned. Yeah, we were all totally in this thing together. While I had high hopes that *he* was perfect, knowing I wasn't stuck with him was reassuring. There was too much new information, too many strange rules and laws and rituals I didn't understand. Knowing I could just say no eased my mind.

"What, exactly is the claiming process?" Katie asked.

Go, Katie, Go!

"And what exactly does it mean to accept his claim? How will we know if we do that? How do we do that, exactly? Is there a wedding ceremony? Do we sign something? Put on a ring? What?"

"You have accepted his claim if you allow your mate, marked or otherwise, the three gifts, the sacred order of three," Officiate Treva clarified. When we all just stared, she tilted her head and sighed. "If you allow your mate to claim your body completely, in all ways."

Katie tilted her own head and raised her dark brow. "Three ways? In some special order? I need details."

Officiate Treva cleared her throat and I couldn't determine if she was laughing, or choking. "Your mouth first, ladies. Followed by your ass. And finally, if you accept him and his claim, he will take you as his mate and place his seed in sacred offering in your womb."

"Oh my god, these people are crazy." Dani swayed beside me and I wrapped my arm around her in a hug.

$\mathcal{L}$*exi*

DANI SHOOK HER HEAD AND SHOVED AT ARM, FORCING ME TO release her from the half hug. "I'm a virgin! And I'm supposed to go anal first? That doesn't seem fair."

Treva must have heard her, for she shook her head and looked at my friend. "No, Danielle. You do not have to, as you say, go anal first. However, if you give your mate the sacred gift of your woman's core, if you accept his claim and his seed in your pussy, he will keep you forever."

"Yeah? What if one of these guys just rapes us then? We're stuck with him forever?" one of the girls asked.

Treva rose to her full height, all traces of kindness gone from her features. "Our Hunters are honored and revered, our most sacred warriors. They would never rape a potential mate."

The girl shook her head, clearly not believing.

Treva put her hands on her hips. "You have each been fitted with an NPU, or neural processing unit, per Interstellar Brides Program protocols. This unit records sensual data and returns it to the Coalition Fleet for analysis and to help place future brides."

I nodded. That was pretty much what Warden Egara had told me.

"If you are violated in any way, come to any of the Officiates at once. The data from your NPU will be examined and the offender executed."

I felt my eyes go wide and Dani's fingers dug into my elbow. "Executed?"

Treva's eyes focused on Dani like lasers. "Yes. We do not tolerate that behavior here. I do not pretend to know what your life was like on Earth, but we are not primitive beasts. Do you all understand? It will not happen. Not here. I give you my word."

As freaked out as I was by her casual talk of executions, her vehemence also made me feel safe. Which was a strange irony I didn't want to think about overmuch.

"Now, it is time for you to join the Everian Hunters who've come to this event in the great hall. They will be eager to see you, and those of you who have dream shared will most likely be able to identify your mate without seeing his palm. If a challenge is issued, your potential mate will be required to prove his worth. You may request to see his mark, or you may choose him without that confirmation. Obviously, it's not too difficult to know the truth when a palm is always visible."

"Challenge? What challenge?" Katie again. God bless her. I had no idea what the hell was going on.

Treva answered. "Any Hunter may make a claim, and fight to be the first to court you."

"But you said it's our choice." Katie frowned at her.

Treva laughed and headed for the door leading to the large room on the other side of the closed metal. "True. And no matter the outcome of the challenge, the choice will remain with you. Often, Hunters accept the challenge with the intention of impressing their new mates with their skill and strength in hand-to-hand combat." Turning, she grinned at all of us. "Hoping you will assume those skills will also be applied in bed."

My mate was probably on the other side of those doors... waiting for me. I wrung my hands together, eager to get on with it. The anticipation and nerves were making me sick to my stomach.

"The last I will share is that before you make your choice, the Officiate will take you and the Hunter to another room where you can spend time together to talk, to help you feel more comfortable so you aren't immediately alone with him."

"I wonder what they're like?" Dani mused aloud. "The Hunters, I mean. We've only been here with these guard guys." What had her dream been like, I wondered?

"Hunters," Treva replied. "Hunters are honorable, protective. They will be very eager for you. I am not familiar with Earth males, but the males here today will be very dominant and extremely possessive."

"A possessive, dominant guy?" the petite blonde asked with a sly grin. "When do we start?"

I glanced at Katie. Most of the girls in the room were as excited and ready as I. I could see it in their eyes, the way they were fidgeting and breathing just a little too fast.

There was a knock on the door and a male guard stuck his head in. "All is ready."

"When does it start?" Treva repeated, then smiled broadly. "Right now."

———

ALEXIS

"ARE YOU SHITTING ME?" KATIE WHISPERED. "WHEN TREVA said eighty, I hadn't really thought she meant *eighty*. There are only twelve of us."

We were standing side by side in the middle of a huge room, Katie on my left. The huge room was a cross between an Earth wedding hall and Hogwarts dining room. The one thing neither of those places could claim was eighty hot men. Every single one of them was gorgeous and the testosterone in the room was worse than I imagined an NFL locker room might be after winning the championship.

I felt like prey, circled and eyed by a group of lethal predators just before they swooped in. All were warriors, I'd heard, men who'd fought the Hive and earned the right to an Interstellar Bride for his mate. Combine that with the mark and these males were well vetted.

Not only did they have to be courageous veterans still serving their planet, but they were all born with a mark that potentially matched their female. A mark that made the two lovers dream of each other. That made them hot and bothered.

I rubbed my thighs together, trying to dull the ache that had only grown since I woke up from my own dream this morning, sweaty and tangled in my nightgown. I'd shared some details with Katie and Dani, but I hadn't told them that the garment had been up about my waist and my hand had been between my thighs. My pussy had been wet. Sticky even. Like right now.

"Do all guys on Everis look like this?" I leaned over and whispered the question to Dani, who stood on my right.

All of them were dressed in identical uniforms. They wore tan-colored pants and shirt with a darker jacket, a chocolate color, on top. Black boots came to below their knees. Just like on US uniforms, braids or stripes of color adorned their wrists or upper arms, indicating rank. Some had no stripes at all, some had one. A few had more. There were also little pins at the collar of their jacket. They were different, depending on the wearer, and I wondered what they signified.

A man in uniform was hot, but to make this bunch even more…virile, were the thigh holsters. None had guns in them, perhaps so they didn't shoot each other when fighting over us—I envisioned a fight easily—but having their strong thighs delineated definitely worked for me.

"I have no idea, but my last date on Earth looked like PeeWee Herman in comparison to these guys," Dani said. I couldn't help but smile, thinking back on the dates I'd had. Dani totally called it. The boys I'd dated were weak shadows of men compared to these Hunters.

"I'm looking at eighty reasons why I'm glad I didn't punch my V card back home," Katie added.

I couldn't help the snort that escaped, but I sobered quickly when two men came our way.

"Earth females," the one with dark hair said. He had two stripes on his sleeve.

I nodded my head.

"Have you shared dreams with a marked mate?" He bowed low, taking my hand in his and placing a soft kiss on my fingers. "Or are you free to be worshipped by another?"

The man beside him had lighter hair and remained quiet. While he seemed content to stand before us, he wasn't as eager. He must be the guy's wingman, obviously convinced none of us were his mate.

"I'm sorry." I pulled my hand free and he stood. "We've all been sharing dreams since we arrived." I kind of felt bad for them, but I had to wonder, if they were so good looking, why didn't they have Everian women climbing them like wild monkeys? I mean, if I didn't have the mark, didn't know there was one specific male here for me, I'd be working the hall.

"Terrible news." He grinned, and I hoped he found his mate. He was charming and fun and hot enough to melt the polar ice caps. But he wasn't mine, and we both knew it. "Should he fail to please you, I beg you to find me. I will lick your sweet cream until you no longer remember his name."

Did he...? Was that...? Did he just tell me he wanted to... God, these guys were full throttle. What was Von going to be like in person?

"Back away, Zakariah. She's mine. I made first claim." A deep voice spoke from behind me and I whirled, thrilled finally to meet the man of my dreams...

Except it wasn't. The strange officer who'd been watching me the last two days stood behind me like a guard dog. What the hell was he talking about. He wasn't mine, either. I glanced quickly from Katie to Dani and both shook their heads. We had no idea what this guy was talking about.

"So be it, Cosmo." The playfulness faded from my flirting friend, Zakariah, and he inclined his head, clearly disappointed, and walked away.

Over the next hour, six of the twelve women left with a male in tow. Some of the males left on their own and all the while the guard named Cosmo stood behind me, watching like a snake. That's what it felt like. Like he was a snake and I the fat little mouse he couldn't wait to swallow hole.

But that was not going to happen. No way. I refused. Not even for thirty days. And besides, Von would come for me. He had to come for me.

When only about ten Hunters remained, Dani leaned her head on my shoulder with a sigh. "I don't think they're going to come. Our mates."

I felt disappointed, but I knew he was here, on this planet. Somewhere. And if he didn't show up? He'd said to wait for him. But for how long? Was I supposed to just remain in this place, dream about him, until—

A set of the hall's double doors opened with such force they slammed into the walls. In came an Everian male with more intent than any of the others. More focus. More... power. He wore the same uniform, but I could see some kind of leaf pins at his collar and four stripes on his sleeves. But that was like sprinkles on a great big chocolate cake. It was his dark hair with striking blue eyes that had me mesmerized. The way he looked about the room, gaze raking over each one of the remaining women until he looked at me. Then never looked away.

His shoulders were broad and I watched as his chest rose and fell with his deep breathing. Had he run here or something? Was that why he was late? The uniform fit him perfectly, especially the taut fit over his strong leg muscles. His hands clenched in fists at his sides as he made his way to me.

Oh. My. God.

"Holy shit, Lexi," Katie murmured. "He's coming straight for you."

7

*L*exi

HE WAS. IT WAS AS IF I HAD A ROPE AND I WAS PULLING HIM IN. A tractor beam out of the sci-fi movies. If I was bringing him to me, then he was capturing me in his stare. I held my breath and I was sure my heart skipped a beat.

"He's so hot," Dani whispered. "I swear he's got pheromones dripping from his pores."

Yeah, he did and I was sucking them all up as if I'd been in a drought. The way my nipples tightened, the way my core clenched, I had to admit I'd never felt like this back home. Not once. I definitely hadn't felt like this by just staring at anyone else before. And he hadn't even talked to me yet.

No, he had talked to me. In my dreams. And then some. I knew it was *him*. Von. Felt it.

When he stopped before me, he stared. I stared back. I couldn't miss the chiseled brow, the piercing blue eyes, the blunt nose, full lips, square jaw, dark stubble. God, the list could go on and on, but either Katie or Dani cleared her throat.

"These are my friends." I said their names, but didn't turn my head. Neither did he.

"Greetings, friends," he said in way of reply. His voice was just as I remembered and I shivered.

Having him two feet in front of me made my dead libido wake up. I wanted to jump on him, kiss him, lick his neck, run my fingers through his hair, then down over his chest and rock-hard abs. Over his cock. God, I wanted to squeeze it in my fist, stroke it. Lick it.

I whimpered.

The corner of his mouth tipped up at the slight sound.

"Will you tell me your name now?" he asked, and I smiled. It was his way of letting me know he was the one in my dreams. No one else would know that detail, no one but *him*.

"Lexi," I whispered.

He repeated it once, then again. Testing it. I loved the sound of it on his tongue. What else would be good on his tongue? Yeah, my nipple.

"Oh my god," I groaned.

One dark brow inched up. "Problem?" he asked.

"I have one." The voice was gruff, loud. It made my mate's face go dark with anger as he finally tore his gaze from mine to look past me, over my shoulder.

"Cosmo."

I finally looked away from my mate's chiseled features and glanced over my shoulder to where Cosmo stood in his navy uniform with Officiate Treva in matching navy beside him.

The tension between the two males was obvious. I didn't like the guy and it was obvious Von didn't either. I was actually glad they weren't friends because that would be awkward. Who wanted to be with a guy who had a creepy best friend?

"You have met Alexis Lopez?" Cosmo asked.

Cosmo knew my name? I hadn't spoken a word to him. Why did he know my name?

Von turned and faced his adversary. "I have met *my mate,* yes."

"Your mate?" Cosmo countered. Anger turned his eyes cold. "Officiate Treva will confirm that I have already made first claim."

I saw Von's fists tighten, felt the anger come off him in waves. "She is mine. I challenge your claim."

What? This Cosmo guy made a claim on me? Was there a sign-up sheet somewhere I didn't know about? He hadn't spoken a single word to me. Shouldn't he have at least asked me first? While I didn't want to get too close to the guy, he could have come to me. Maybe he'd tried? I had to admit, if he'd been trying, I hadn't made it easy for him. Every time the three of us saw him approaching the last two days, we would spin around and walk the other way. Maybe I should have sucked it up and talked to him, let him try, because I could have shut this shit down pretty fast with a big fat no.

"She is mine." Cosmo's voice seemed to lower an octave and the sound of his dark declaration made me shiver, and not with desire, if that was his goal.

"You cannot refuse my challenge. She's my *marked* mate," Von growled.

"What?" Cosmo was livid, his face turning a mottled shade of red. Wow, he really wanted me. I'd always wanted to be sexy and desirable enough that two guys might fight over me, but I realized that was not a good fantasy. These two men were powerful warriors, and they looked like they were ready to rip each other to pieces with me standing between them.

"We have dream shared, our marks match," Von added, looking at Treva now. Obviously this clarified everything, to everyone but me.

"Is this true?" Treva asked me, her gaze steady but emotionless. It seemed she was the impartial judge in this face-off.

I nodded. "Yes."

"Major Cosmo, as you are well aware, the law states that the female will choose which warrior will receive first rights, and thirty days to officially mate," she said, sounding as if she was reciting from some legal rule book. She probably was.

Out of the corner of my eye, I saw Katie's shoulders relax. Clearly she had been worried I'd have to go off with creepy guy, too.

"I demand a combat challenge," Major Cosmo barked. He turned to me. "You must accept the winner of the challenge as your first."

"No." The word whispered over my lips like a soft sigh. No way. And what was Cosmo's problem? Was he not backing down because he really wanted me or because he didn't want Von to have me? There appeared to be no love lost between the two of them and I didn't want to get caught in the middle of their fight.

Von growled, his body crowding me. His hand came to rest on the small of my back, but instead of feeling intimidated, like Cosmo made me feel, I felt protected by Von's aggressive posture, his touch. His strength. An odd sense of comfort washed over me and I swayed toward Von, wanting more of his heat, his nearness.

Cosmo watched me move and his eyes narrowed. I

shivered as Von gently pulled me to stand behind him where Cosmo could no longer see me.

"You have no choice, Cosmo. You must accept Von's challenge," Officiate Treva ordered.

Von turned to look at me for a moment and I forgot to breathe. I saw so much hunger in his gaze, such awe. His gaze fell from mine and I knew he was staring at my right breast.

I didn't want to watch some stupid fight where Von and Cosmo would beat each other to death. That was crazy. I peeked around Von and spoke to the Officiate. "Treva, I would like to see proof of Von's mark before I choose him."

"Doesn't she understand how this works?" Cosmo asked. "Von, show her your damn palm."

Von glanced at me. "My mark is elsewhere."

Treva's eyes widened and Cosmo appeared to have been hit in the head with a bat. "Elsewhere?" he asked.

"I was not born with the mark on my palm," Von replied, although I knew that. I knew it because my own mark tingled on my chest. Did his as well?

"This is quite unusual," Treva replied. "You must both reveal your marks then to confirm the match."

"Here?" I squeaked, thinking about having to expose my breast to the entire room.

"Is there a problem? You made the request," she replied.

Von stepped between us and spoke to her. "I am aware of the protocols, Officiate Treva, but Lexi's mark is on a place I do not wish other males to see."

I blushed and my nipples tightened as he watched, as if answering his silent call. He lifted his hand, as if to touch me, but stopped himself and moved to block Cosmo's view completely once more. Treva had said they were possessive and protective, hadn't she? I just hadn't realized how much Von's all-male posturing would turn me on.

Officiate Treva looked at me. "Follow me to a private room."

Von looked at me again, nodded. His jaw was clenched. He didn't like what was happening, didn't like the way Cosmo lurked or looked at me, but it seemed he couldn't argue further. And I had no desire to see his beautiful chiseled face marred by bruises and blood.

Treva walked to me. "Alexis, if you will accompany me?"

I glanced at Katie and Dani, bit my lip. Katie shrugged and Dani nodded, a reassuring smile on her face.

I didn't have a choice but to follow. If I wanted Von, I'd have to play by their rules. I'd initiated this to try to stop a fight, but judging by the way the two men were scowling at one another, this wasn't going to matter. Nothing would dissuade Cosmo.

Maybe he didn't want me at all. Maybe he just wanted an excuse to fight Von.

Treva led the way. I was behind her and the two men followed. Looking back, I peeked around their large frames and saw Katie and Dani giving me thumbs-up signs until the door to the main hall closed behind us. Treva led us to a side room, a much smaller one. I heard the door click shut.

"Are you aware of the mark on your body, Alexis?" Treva asked.

I nodded, then whispered, "Yes."

My gaze flicked to Von, who was watching me with coiled tension.

"Senior Hunter Von mentioned it is not on your palm, but in a private location?"

I nodded again. When none spoke, I realized they were waiting for more from me. "The side of my breast."

Major Cosmo's nostrils flared and Von's blue eyes darkened to a stormy gray.

He stepped forward, stripped off his brown uniform jacket, dropped it to the floor. Unbuttoning his shirt, he tugged the side of it open to reveal part of a drool-worthy chest. There was a smattering of dark hair and a flat nipple. Beside it, on the side of his ribs was his mark. A mark identical to my own. I gasped, seeing the upside-down Texas-shaped discoloration on his flesh was fascinating. I wanted to touch it. Kiss it. Trace it with my tongue. I could even feel my mark tingle beneath my dress. A proximity thing?

"Her body is for me and me alone." Von's words sliced through the silence, raising his eyebrows as if daring Officiate Treva to argue.

She pressed some kind of communication unit strapped to her thigh. "This is highly unusual. I have never, in all my years in this role, seen this. Senior Hunter Von's mark is not on his palm, but has been witnessed and confirmed," she said, clearly for a record of some sort.

"I want to see *her* mark for myself," Major Cosmo countered. "My claim is first."

"Not if you are denied by the female," Treva countered, her ball-buster voice back in full force. Thank god.

I inwardly sighed then, relieved to hear the rule allowing me to kick him in the balls if I wanted to in case he didn't back off. The tone of her response had me thinking she wasn't too keen on the guy.

"I'm not flashing either man," I said.

"You don't have to."

"Officiate—"

"Major Cosmo."

They both spoke at the same time, but Treva gave a

withering look to the major. "At your high rank, you should be familiar with protocol. For Alexis's benefit, and perhaps yours—" She gave him a pointed look. "I will share them."

She looked to me.

"As a representative of the Touchstone, I am the only one required to witness proof of the marks on both you and your potential mate's palms. I record the confirmation. My word is law and will validate the marked match. In this *highly* unusual case, I will be the one to witness the proof. No one else needs to see it, Alexis, unless you allow it. Do you choose to allow these men to view your mark?"

After a quick glance at Major Creepy, I looked to Von. I knew he wanted to see my breast and I actually wanted to show him. He'd touched it, kissed it in the dream last night. Since I knew we were matched and I wasn't going to deny him, he would see it in real life soon enough. But not now. Not like this. I didn't want the first time he looked at my body to be in a proving room with others watching.

"No. I prefer to be alone."

She offered a curt nod as reply. "Hunters, please wait outside."

Von waited for the major to leave the room before he followed, but stopped before me. The heated look he gave me was scorching. "This is a formality only. Soon you will be mine. It is now my turn."

I frowned, unsure of what he meant.

"My turn to wait for you."

He was saying his words from our dream.

Without touching me—although his gaze felt like a lover's caress—he left, ensuring the door was closed firmly behind him.

"I've seen many marked mates before, but I've never seen

64

a male so…intent," Treva said as I continued to stare at the door.

"You believe we are marked mates?" I asked.

"I have no doubt. But Major Cosmo does. You are very popular, it seems."

I looked to her, saw her not as the official in the fancy uniform, but as a female.

"I have never had two guys into me before," I admitted. "I thought it would be pretty cool, especially when both of them are really hot."

"Cool? Hot? Is there a temperature problem on Earth?"

I had to laugh, and it made me feel better. "Sorry. I guess those NPU things that translate for us don't understand slang. I thought I would enjoy having attractive men fight over me, but I've changed my mind. They are powerful and dangerous."

She offered me a smile. "Yes, all Everian Hunters are. Your mate, especially. Now show me this mark of yours."

I slid the strap of my dress off my shoulder, pushed it down so that it exposed my right breast. Lifting my hand, I cupped it, covering much of it except for the side, which curved outward. The mark was clearly visible to her.

"Thank you."

I pulled the dress back into place.

"Ready for them to return?"

I was ready for Von to return, but knew the major wouldn't be far behind. "Yes."

She opened the door and Von came in, looking me over from head to toe as if to make sure I hadn't been hurt. The major came in, crossed his arms over his chest.

Treva pressed a button on her thigh again. "Alexis Lopez's mark has been witnessed and confirmed as an exact match to

Senior Hunter Von. Let the record show that they are marked mates."

She turned to me and the look in her eyes made me freeze in place, barely daring to breathe. "Alexis Lopez, do you accept Major Cosmo's claim?"

"No. I do not."

"Do you accept Senior Hunter Von's claim?"

I could feel Von's eyes on me and my body responded as if he were a blazing sun kissing my flesh with warmth and light. I was so hot, so eager to turn to him and finally know what it felt like to touch him. "Yes. I accept Von."

Officiate Treva spoke into her recording thing again. "Alexis Lopez of Earth has chosen Senior Hunter Von as her first claim. The thirty days afforded the female to accept or reject her new mate begins now."

He looked at me, and if I'd been wearing panties, they would have melted right off my body. "It won't take that long."

Her clear gaze shifted. "Senior Hunter Von, please be aware that your mate is untouched. You have thirty days to claim her virginities or return her to the care of another here at the Touchstone."

He nodded and held out his hand to me.

The major, Cosmo, looked like he was going to punch a hole in the wall, but there was nothing he could do. Thankfully.

"I am done waiting, mate," Von said, his voice rough. Just like in the dream. I shivered and took his hand, felt the hot tingle up my arm. This was the first time we touched. His skin was soft, his caress almost hot. I felt callouses I remembered from the dreams. I didn't want to let go.

He pulled me from the room and I thought over what Treva had said and recorded.

"Wait." I stopped and Von yanked my arm before he, too, could stop. Looking down at me, he stroked a finger over my cheek.

"Yes, mate?"

"Virginities?"

on

I HELD HER HAND. MY BRIDE. MY MARKED MATE. HER LONG black hair fell in a dark curtain halfway down her back, the strands shimmering in the light. Her eyes were lined with accent that drew attention, making them the focus of her beautiful face. She was small, not reaching my shoulder, but her full breasts and flared hips were those of a woman ripe for the taking. Every curve was outlined by a flowing red gown. If the Officiates had followed standard protocol, she would be naked beneath.

She'd been waiting for me, just as I'd told her to do. In the room with the other females and a number of men, she'd stood out like a space beacon. It had taken only seconds to find her. Her perfect curves, her dark hair, her wary and eager gaze catching mine.

That fact alone made my cock hard and my mind spin

with possibilities for the evening. I would court her properly, share a meal with her, get to know her and give her time to adjust to me.

But I could not afford to wait to begin claiming her. Not with Cosmo eager to take my place in her bed. I needed my Lexi tied to me, bonded and fucked and claimed so fools like Cosmo would understand the truth.

Lexi was mine.

Her mouth. Her ass. Her virgin pussy. They were all mine and I was not a man inclined to share. But by her one-word question, it seemed she didn't know everything about what would happen next, or the sensual ways I would claim her body.

"Virginities?" she repeated. "I just didn't think it was true."

The hallway was quiet, only a few others about. Now that Lexi was a matched mate and we were officially within the thirty days of her claiming period, the other males kept their distance. They knew intervening would easily mean severe injury. Occasionally, challenges resulted in one of the Hunters' deaths. I wouldn't hesitate to take down anyone who got in my way.

Most Hunters stayed away from marked mates, the rare and sacred nature of the bond something all Hunters dreamed of. Men with honor allowed the marked Hunter to woo his bride, to do his best to win her heart without interference or trouble.

But Cosmo was not honorable, at least not when it came to me. The challenge would occur, and he would kill me if he could. Kill me and take what was mine.

That I could not allow. And I did not fear the major. We'd battled one another many times. I always won. I would crush him like an insect beneath my boot before I allowed him to touch my mate.

"Von? Did you hear me?"

"Yes, mate. I heard you. Virginities. There are three," I said. I did nothing to hide the evidence of my desire for my mate, at the thought of claiming all three of her holes. I never wanted her to doubt how much I wanted her. Needed her. Holding out a hand, I held back a cheer when she placed her much smaller one in my own.

"On Earth your pussy is the only virginity you claim?"

"Well, I guess if you have anal sex you're no longer an anal virgin, but it's not really the one people think of for their wedding night. Or… whatever," she replied and her cheeks turned a delightful blushing pink. I wondered what thoughts occupied her mind. Perhaps my innocent little virgin had thoughts that were not exactly *innocent*. I couldn't wait to find out.

"Here on Everis, we follow the sacred order of three, if we can. It allows your mate to prove his desire for you, and demonstrate his ability to bring you tremendous pleasure."

"Treva spoke of it quite clearly." She blushed then.

Slowly, so as not to scare her, I leaned forward and brushed my lips against hers. "I will claim you here, first, mate. Your mouth. As you will have mine…" I trailed kisses over her cheekbone to her ear. "…everywhere."

Her shudder made me smile, but it was the way her body swayed toward me that made my cock jump in anticipation. Gods, she was perfect. So sensual. So sensitive to my slightest touch. I would rule her body, make it mine.

Gathering her close, I kissed her again, my arms sliding down her curves as my tongue plunged deep, stroking hers until she moaned, her nipples hard pebbles pressed to my chest. "I will take you here, second." I squeezed her bottom gently, pulling her soft body flush with mine so she couldn't help but feel my erection between us, the hard cock I would use to fuck her virgin ass. "I will slide my cock inside your body, little mate, and you will pant and moan and writhe beneath me, begging for more."

"Oh my god." Lexi tore her mouth from mine and pressed her hands on my chest, pushing away so she could look up at me. "I can't. I mean, I never. I..."

Her words faded as she stared up at me. I loosened my hold on her bottom and let her have breathing room, but she didn't pull away, and the primitive part of me reveled in the knowledge that already her body craved contact with mine.

I held her gaze as I continued. "Your true virginity, your hot, wet core, is a prize I have not yet earned, my beautiful mate."

"I don't understand this. Why do you do this? Why not just..."

"Fuck?" The crude word left my mouth and her eyes darkened. She licked her lips and I knew if I didn't get her out of this hallway, I'd start claiming that sweet mouth right here.

"Yes."

"Did you like sharing dreams with me? Like me kissing you, touching your breast, suckling your nipple?" I lowered my voice so it was more intimate. This conversation shouldn't be for a Touchstone hallway, but I doubted she'd continue walking with me until she had the answers she sought.

"Yes." She glanced up at me through her dark lashes. "I can't lie to you."

"No," I said instantly. "Every emotion shows on your face. I will know if you lie. But why would you want to? There are no secrets between mates. Between us."

She nodded. While my balls ached knowing the extent of

her innocence and my interest in being the one to enlighten her, in this moment it would have been helpful for her to be a little *less* naive as to what we'd do together.

"Do you trust me?"

"I don't know you," she countered.

"You do. Our minds have touched, mate. You know me," I repeated.

She studied me for a moment. "I think so. Yes."

"Then know this, I will claim you in the sacred way. I will prove my worth to you. I will prove that I can love you, adore you, bring you unimaginable pleasure before I ask for your most sacred gift."

"My virginity?"

"The right to lay my seed within you and pray it takes root. The right to care for you and protect you and our children until my death. Your trust. Your love. I want everything, Lexi."

"You want a baby?"

I grinned. I couldn't help it, not with the shocked look on her face. "I'd like many children, mate. As many as you would gift to me."

Her smile faded. "What if I can't have kids?"

I lifted my hand and touched her cheek gently. "Then I will be honored and pleased to be gifted with you. I need nothing else."

She lifted on tiptoe to kiss me, a quick, chaste kiss on the lips. But it meant more to me than any battle I'd ever won fighting in the war. Her shy smile made something hard and cold unravel in my chest and pain lanced behind my eyes. Years of loneliness and bleak, barren days melted under that kiss. I quickly turned away, blinking hard, else the pain of my soul coming back to life would manifest on my cheeks.

A Hunter did not cry simply because a beautiful woman pressed an innocent kiss to one's lips.

"I don't know what to do. You'll have to tell me what to do."

Stepping back, I reached for her hand. I needed distance, time to adjust to the heavy, painful weight settling in my chest where I'd been dead and empty for so long. "I've got you, love. Are you hungry?"

"Hungry?" She seemed confused by the change of topic. "Yes."

"Then I shall feed you."

"But I thought—"

"I will not claim you here in the hallway, Lexi. I will not claim any of your virginities until you are ready."

She had thirty days. It was my job to make it happen sooner. Starting tonight. Starting right now.

With her small hand wrapped around my arm, I escorted her to the dining halls. The Touchstone had a large community dining room used by the officers, unclaimed females and Officiates. It was large, public and very safe for the potential mates.

But on the upper level, private dining quarters had been built to accommodate the needs of warriors who came here to seduce and claim their brides. Men like me.

The Officiate stood at attention in his blue uniform. "Senior Hunter Von, greetings."

"Is my room ready?" I'd known she was here, known she would be mine. I'd also known she might be nervous and most certainly hungry at some point today. It was private and not my own room. The perfect place for her to relax and enjoy being together. If it led to more—which it would since I knew we were more than just marked, we were matched— it would be private.

"Of course, of course." He bowed low to my mate, which earned him my gratitude, and swung his arm to indicate the direction we would go. "If you would follow me, my lady."

The man led and I followed behind Lexi as she fell in step behind him. Abruptly, he halted and Lexi nearly slammed into the man's back.

Wrapping my arm around her waist, I pulled her back against me just in time.

"No! You will not take her upstairs!" Cosmo's voice boomed over the suddenly quiet dining hall and Lexi jolted at the loud, aggressive sound.

"Hush. I've got this, love," I whispered in her ear and kissed her temple before gently moving her behind me. One of my men had used his Hunter's speed to appear at my side and I placed Lexi behind me where I knew my friend could protect her if something should happen here. Now.

I did not want to answer this challenge. Cosmo's was a fool's plight, yet his pride would not allow him to back down. I understood, but more than anything, I wanted Lexi in my arms, the taste of her sweet cream coating my tongue, her soft cries of release in my ears. I wanted the wet heat of her mouth stretched wide around my cock.

I wanted *her*. Not this. "Leave it be, Cosmo. She's mine."

Cosmo lifted the man before him by the shoulders and set him aside as if the full-grown Everian weighed no more than a child's doll. Cosmo was a Hunter, like me. His strength and speed enhanced by his rage, his desire for what was mine, for revenge.

He was drunk and in pain. He didn't truly want my mate. He wanted to hurt me, to take something precious from me, as he believed I'd done to him.

"I hate you, Von. You will not claim her. Not until you answer to me." Cosmo practically roared his demands and I heard Lexi's gasp behind me. Her fear acted as acid on my patience, burning it away between one heartbeat and the next.

on

"LEAVE NOW, OR I WILL BREAK YOU. WALK AWAY, COSMO. Leave it be."

"You know I can't." Cosmo glowered as he walked past me. I followed his movements, placing myself between him and my mate at all times. I didn't rest easy until he was gone, out of the restaurant and out of sight. Tomorrow was soon enough to deal with him. Tonight, I wanted to focus on my mate.

Lexi moved to me, her eyes wide, her face flushed. "What is his problem? You two have bad blood?"

I shook my head. Bad blood? There was nothing wrong with my blood. I nodded my thanks to my friend from home and he disappeared back into the main dining hall as silently as he'd arrived. Not for the first time, I was grateful for the men, the friends and fellow warriors who guarded my back. "My blood is fine, Lexi."

She grinned, clearly amused at something I said even as I fought to get the Hunter within me under control. My instincts raged at me to chase Cosmo down and kill him for threatening my mate. But I was more than my instincts, I was a man, a man very much in need of the soft, feminine touch of the female standing before him.

"That's not what I meant, Von. It's an Earth saying. It means you two have history together, something happened in your past that made you enemies."

"I don't want to talk about Cosmo. Not tonight." I ran my fingertips lightly over her cheek because I couldn't seem to stop touching her.

She looked up at me, studied me, her dark eyes near to piercing my soul, but she inclined her head. When I held out my arm for her once more, she wrapped her small hand around my elbow so we could follow the host upstairs to our private dining room.

"Okay, Von. For tonight." Lexi's hand tightened on my arm, but I covered it with my own, allowed my heat and confidence to comfort her through the small touch. She responded at once, relaxing next to me as we followed the large man to the private dining room I'd reserved. I'd heard that Viken males had seed power, a chemical in their seed that made them and their mate constantly aroused to help with claiming.

Everians didn't have that. We had the marks and their ability to make the chemistry between mates so intense that they were unbelievably attracted and eager for each other. I hadn't believed it before, but I did now. I wanted Lexi with a ferocity that grew each moment I was in her presence. The way she responded to me, it was working on her as well. It seemed to have become even more intense when I'd nuzzled her mark in the dream the night before.

Our host held a chair for my mate, but I shooed him away. Doing this was my honor, my privilege. I would not share her, not even in this small thing. She was mine to treasure, to care for.

With a raised brow, the Officiate hurried to the door. "Senior Hunter Von, are you aware of the dining protocols?" He lifted his hand to the wall, flipping a switch near the door from the left to the right. The switch itself turned from yellow to red. "Yellow is for dining service. Red for privacy."

I nodded but said nothing as he moved the switch back to yellow and left us alone, the door sliding closed behind him.

The room was small, but more than adequate for my needs. A round table rested near one wall. Delicate dining service, gold utensils, tall glasses for wine or ale and beautiful crystalline lights created an intimate experience for couples to get to know one another. The chairs were plush, a soft green that made me think of forests and living things. Of life outside this artificial fortress.

I walked to a chair and held it out for my mate, pleased when she sat at once. The back of it rested just below her shoulders, and I took advantage of the moment to lean over and place a chaste kiss on her exposed shoulder.

She gasped at the contact and I longed to do it again, to hear her moan. I didn't dare linger, but took my place opposite her as the first course of sweetened fruit and cheeses was brought in with wine.

My mate ate like a bird, barely picking at the food that melted on the tongue like soft candy.

"Alexis Lopez. Tell me about your life. I want to know everything about you."

Her eyes darted to mine, and she took a deep breath. "I'm boring. I swear."

"Not to me." I put my utensils down and leaned forward,

focused, intent on anything she would tell me, any truth she may reveal. She was mine, and I wanted to know everything.

A small smile was my reward and she placed her hands in her lap, her fingers dancing over one another with her anxiety. I wanted to pull her into my lap and pet her, kiss and hold her until she forgot to be nervous. Until there was nothing but her...and me.

"I turned twenty-one a couple weeks ago. I was supposed to finish college, but my dad died last year and I didn't have time to apply for financial aid, so I had to take a semester off. I just never went back."

"What is college?" Some of what she said I understood, but not all.

She opened her mouth, frowned, tilted her head to look at me. "Wow. Okay. Ummm, college is a place of higher learning, a place to receive education and training for a special job, like how to run a business, or how to be a doctor, engineering and computer programming. Stuff like that."

"And what were you studying to become?"

She shrugged. "I don't know. I thought I wanted to go into graphic design, but I don't like drawing on a computer. I prefer pen and paper. And there just isn't any money in art, unless you get lucky or are some kind of genius."

"And you need money on your world?"

Glass of wine halfway to her lips, she paused to stare at me with round eyes. "Yes. Don't you?"

"Barter and trade is a primitive social structure."

She laughed. "I am so on an alien world right now." She sipped the wine, set the glass down and licked her lips. I wanted to lick those lips. "So, if you don't have money, how do you pay for things? Buy things? Where do you live?"

"I am a Hunter."

"I don't know what that means. What do you do? Kill animals to eat?"

"No. I enforce the laws on our world."

"So, you're a cop?" Fingernails drumming the table, she frowned. "How did I end up mated to a cop?"

"I do not know your word *cop*, but I am one of the Hunters assigned to maintain order on Everis. I hunt criminals, determine punishment for crimes, settle disputes between parties in my region. Should a convicted criminal escape prison, I would hunt him and bring him to swift and final justice. Is that what your cop does?"

"Hell, no." She stared at me, her gaze holding mine as if she were trying to see into my soul. I let her look. "So, you're more like police, detective, judge and jury in one?"

I considered her words carefully. "Yes. We are highly respected. Most of us served, fighting in the Hive wars before being assigned to the Hunter forces. I am a Senior Hunter of the forces in this region. But my authority is respected anywhere on the planet, or within the Coalition Fleet. We have been called upon to track criminals to other worlds. Our tracking skills are legendary, and we are often hired by leaders of other planets to hunt their criminals and bring them to justice."

"How do you track someone? Do you have special Spidey-sense or something?"

Spidey-sense? "I cannot explain it to you, mate. But know this, Hunters use instincts older than our race in pursuit of our prey. I can't describe the feeling to you, but if I focus my thoughts on a person, on a criminal or a thing, eventually, I will find that which I seek. Even if I have to travel across worlds."

"Wow. You're a total badass." Her words were barely more than a whisper and her pulse raced at the base of her neck.

"I am not an ass. I am a Hunter. And now, *I am yours*, Lexi. I will never leave your side, never betray you. I will kill to protect you, and avenge any who wrong you or bring you dishonor. I will bring you pleasure you can't imagine, fulfill every fantasy and desire if you but ask. You are mine, mate. And I take care of what's mine."

"All because we share a mark?"

"Yes."

The server refilled both of our cups and I watched, amused, as Lexi took a long drink, emptying nearly half the glass. The slight tremble in her hand worsened to a noticeable shaking.

"Are you nervous, mate?"

Lexi replaced the glass on the table very careful not so spill. "No. Yes. I don't know." Her gaze darted across the room to the long, green settee draped with assorted pillows, blankets and binding scarves. "I just don't know what to expect. I don't know what you want from me."

"Yes, you do."

Her cheeks heated to a dark pink once more and she bit her full lower lip in a move that forced me to readjust my cock in my pants. "I do, but I've never felt like this before. What we share, this...heat, is overwhelming. I don't know what to do or what to say. I just don't know. I don't want to disappoint you."

I loved her honesty, loved that she was just as eager for me. But I was not an innocent. I knew exactly what would come next and I wasn't fearful. I was almost frantic for her. I had to go slow and enjoy the awakening.

Instead of answering her, I rose and walked to the door, flipping the switch to indicate we were in need of privacy. It was time to claim what was mine.

———

Von

I PULLED LEXI TO HER FEET. STANDING BEFORE ME, SHE trembled with innocence, with fear of the unknown. Not of me.

She was so small and soft and curved and perfect. So ripe. I was sure I could smell the wet welcome between her legs, the musky scent of her wet pussy. Her mind might not know what to expect, but her body was ready.

Lifting my hands to cup her face, I lowered my head and claimed her lips. The taste of her an explosion of wine and sweets and woman on my tongue. She gasped and I took advantage, pushing my tongue into her mouth to explore and conquer, to claim.

"Do not be afraid. I showed you in the dreams what it would be like between us. Do you want more?"

Her hands came to my forearms and I barely heard her. "Yes."

I growled in possessiveness. She was telling me yes, giving me permission to please us both, to take the first step toward making her mine. To claiming her.

"This mouth, love. This mouth is mine." I kissed the side of it, tugged her bottom lip between my teeth before sucking it into my mouth, tasting, exploring, rubbing and suckling until her knees buckled. Arms around her waist, I held her upright and continued to kiss her. Her lips. Her cheek. Her brow. Her nose. Her jaw. "Mine to claim with my kisses, with my cock."

"Oh god," she whimpered.

"Do you like that idea?" I kissed along her jaw, nibbled on her earlobe. Nipped it.

She shivered again. "Yes,"

"You like the idea of licking the pre-cum off the head? You want to swirl your tongue around me, learn my taste, my shape? Then open those lips nice and wide and take my cock nice and deep?"

She licked her lips and my cock pulsed painfully in my pants.

"I do. I want to see it, feel it in my hands."

I stepped back, tugged at the front of my uniform pants, pulled my eager cock free so she could see it.

"Your first cock?"

She nodded and reached out, then stilled, her fingers a few inches away.

I jerked my hips involuntarily.

"Touch me."

She didn't need more permission than that. Her dainty fingers stroked over the head, slipped through the stream of pre-cum oozing from the tip.

"This is crazy," she said, her eyes focused on what her fingers were doing.

I was gritting my teeth, trying not to come, to spurt all over her hand because I was too eager. Damn, she was too fucking hot and this was only her fingertips. When I got in that hot little mouth, I wasn't going to last.

"We've just met and your dick is out and I'm touching it and I shouldn't be this excited for you and—"

"Is your pussy wet?" I asked, cutting off her words. I needed her mind focused on what she wanted, not on what she thought she should be doing.

I watched her shift her weight from foot to foot and I

knew her clit had to be aching. Surely her juices were sliding hotly down her thighs.

She nodded.

"Do you know what it does to me when you tell me that?" I asked.

Her fingers tightened around the head of my cock. "I think I have an idea. Does fluid always come out like this?"

"That's all for you, love. Knowing that's going to be in your mouth soon has my balls so tight. Cup them, see what I mean."

Her hand slipped away and I hissed out a breath at the loss. But then I groaned when she did as I said and my balls were cupped in her palm. When she began to play with them, I had to step back.

"Did I hurt you?" she asked.

Slowly, I shook my head. "It's your turn."

She frowned.

"I'm going to do what I've been dreaming of, even when I'm awake. I'm going to lick up all that juice that's coating your pussy, then suck your clit until you scream, make you come all over my face."

She flushed hotly, not in embarrassment, but in eagerness.

"I see you like that idea."

She nodded again, finally becoming emboldened, perhaps knowing this wasn't all about me. In actuality, it was all about her. My mate would always come once, if not twice, before I ever got my cock inside her. Then several times after that. I would always see to her pleasure first.

Having my cock out, letting her play with it, learn it, before she got on her knees was to put her at ease, to make her hot and eager.

Making her come first? It was my pleasure to do it and then she'd be sated and frantic for more. For my cock.

"After you come, then you'll be all ready for my cock between those lush lips. It'll be time to fill that virgin mouth, to have you swallow down my seed."

She moaned and the sweet sound had me stepping close to her again, my cock pressing against her belly. Her head fell back on her shoulders as I kissed my way down her neck.

"If you suck me hard, mate, claim my cock for your own, I will give you a reward. Once I come in that sweet mouth, I'll fuck you with my tongue until you can't breathe, until your clit is so sensitive one flick of my tongue will make your hot little pussy flutter and spasm, desperate to be filled."

When I reached her ear, I told her the rest. "Don't worry, this is all we'll do tonight. But you'll want more. You might even beg me for it."

She shifted her hips into mine, an action I doubt she even knew she made.

"Soon, your ass will be mine, mate. I'm going to stretch you open, get you so desperate for me that you beg me to take you, and then I'm going to fuck that virgin hole slow and hard and deep. I'm going to fill you with my cock, play with your nipples, rub your clit as I fuck you and make you come over and over again."

"Oh god."

"But not tonight. Tonight, I'll take that virgin mouth and learn your taste."

"Von," she murmured.

Fuck. I loved to hear my name from those lips.

Her nipples were hard pebbles against my chest and her breathing came in soft, rapid huffs as I cupped her ass with my hands and pulled her up onto her tiptoes, until her sex rested against my hard cock. "And then, when you are ready to be mine forever, I'm going to fuck your hot, wet, virgin pussy until you can't remember your own name, until you're screaming mine, begging me to fill you up, begging me to fuck you raw, fill you with my seed, put my baby in your womb, make you mine forever."

"You're really good at this."

"What?"

"Dirty talk."

I grinned. "You like it when I tell you what I'm going to do to you?"

"Yes."

"There's one word I want to hear, love."

She knew it instinctively, for she didn't pause, didn't even think.

"Please."

Yes, that was it. Submissive and begging.

One word, and my control snapped.

10

on

I LIFTED HER FROM THE FLOOR AND CARRIED HER TO THE cushioned settee lining the wall. I knew no one would enter and I knew that I wasn't the first Everian male to use the room to sate his need.

With one hand between her breasts, I laid her back like an offering to the Divine. Except she wasn't offering her lush curves to any god, she was offering them to me.

Her dark hair spread out beneath her, a striking contrast to the pale green cloth, and I stood over her, admiring the exotic beauty that was mine now. Part of me wanted to rush like a wild man, to conquer in a frantic lunge to victory.

But more, I needed to savor this moment, commit the vision before me to memory so I would never forget the way she looked this first time. I'd been alone a long damn time, never thought to have this deep connection, a marked mate.

But the fire pumping through my veins would not be

denied. My mark pulsed with life, filling me with need. Lust. Obsession. I would never get enough of her.

Slowly, so as not to frighten her, I dropped to my knees, gripped her ankles and tugged her so her ass was at the very edge. I ran my hands up her legs, to her knees, applying gentle pressure to open her for me. Dropping my head, I kissed the inside of one knee, then the other, her feet dangling over onto the floor. I ran my hands up her soft thighs, gathered the soft folds of her gown in my hands as I went.

Her scent hit me like a bludgeon and my mind went blank, my cock jumped. Hunter's instinct took over, a primitive side of my nature I rarely used. And my base desires were focused on one thing, not prey, but her.

My mate.

Before me was her virgin pussy. She'd come up on her elbows and looked down her delectable body at me.

"Von," she whispered.

No one had ever seen her like this before. Passion-filled eyes, ragged breaths, tight nipples, parted thighs, her perfect pink pussy exposed to me.

"Are all Earth females bare?"

She frowned and looked down at herself. "I am bare. Is this what you wanted?"

I breathed deeply again, her scent intoxicating. With a shaky finger, I ran it along her slit, felt the silky heat of her as it coated my skin. Lifting it to my lips, I tasted her for the first time.

"All mates are bare. You'll see why. You're going to be so sensitive for me." I touched her again.

"Von."

I needed more of her flavor on my tongue. That sample hadn't been enough. I had to taste her.

I gave her no more time to prepare, no warning, simply lowered my mouth to her cream and licked, hard, through the plump folds.

Lexi whimpered, but held her legs open when I released them to move my hands to her pussy.

Another lick and her hands were in my hair, tugging. "Von."

Yes. That's what I wanted to hear.

"You may say my name, mate. But nothing else. If you say anything else, I will stop. Do you understand, Lexi? My name. I want to hear *my* name."

"Please."

I nipped the inside of her thigh. "My name, Lexi. Only my name."

"Von." Her hips shifted beneath me as she attempted to force my return to her core. "Von."

The first was a demand. The second a plea. My cock throbbed, eager to feel her hot, wet mouth, those firm innocent lips. I wanted to feel her swallow me deep into her throat. I wanted her to take all of me, lave me with her tongue and lips and drink every drop of my cum.

But first, I needed her so desperate, so needy, that her eyes would glaze over and her mind would shut off. I needed her ready to accept pleasure. Hers. Mine. Ours.

Slowly, I worked just one finger inside her as I licked and sucked her sensitive nub. Careful not to break the virginal barrier I felt, the proof of her innocence that made me snarl and redouble my efforts to make her scream.

Her orgasm would be mine. Her pussy was mine. Her clit was mine. Every inch of her creamy flesh was mine.

Mine.

I pushed one finger into her body, curved it slightly to seek the special place inside her that would drive her wild.

With my mouth, I worked her clit, licking, sucking, humming, as she squirmed and bucked beneath me. My free hand, I lifted to cup a full breast, to squeeze and tug on her nipple as I worked her with my mouth.

Her whimpers escalated to moans, then…

"Please."

I stopped moving and she whimpered. "God. No. Von. Please." She tugged on my hair, her hands in fists. "Von. Von. Von."

I used my mouth to reward her each time she spoke my name, and soon, her pussy clamped down on my finger in a spasm that had her arching her back with a long, keening cry.

Showing no mercy, I controlled her release with finger and tongue, rode her orgasm, drawing it out.

When it was over, I gave her no rest, working her again until she was whimpering, thrashing about, desperate for more. On the edge.

With deliberate slowness, I stood, then pulled my finger inch by slow inch from her pussy as she focused on my face.

Her eyes dark and expressive, she stared up at me with complete trust, absolute surrender, and I knew it was time to take what was mine.

"Do you want another orgasm, mate?" I wiped my slick lips with the back of my hand. The scent of her was on my mouth, my finger. "Do you want me to work you with my lips and tongue again until your wet pussy clamps down on me like a fist, squeezing me? Do you want me to make you scream?"

She licked her lips. Nodded. "I love your dirty talk."

"I want something, too. Do you remember what it is?"

"My virgin mouth?" She sat up, her knees still parted, her pussy still exposed and reached for the buckle of my pants. I didn't stop her. In moments, she pulled my hard cock free, wrapped her hands around it, rubbed the pre-cum from the tip and lifted the drop of liquid to her hot little mouth. I nearly came as she licked her finger clean, sucked it into her mouth and squeezed the head of my cock with her other hand.

I wanted just to tilt my hips, slide my cock into her virgin pussy right now. It was *right* there. But no. It wasn't the time for that. It was time to take that mouth.

Her gaze lifted from my cock to my face, but I did not issue commands. This she had to choose on her own. I wanted those lips to wrap around me more than I wanted my next breath, but I would not force her, or rush her.

As her mate, it was my job to seduce her, to make her an eager and willing participant in our sex games. She was mine to protect, to teach, to claim. I would show her nothing but pleasure.

She stared up at me for long seconds, the tension in my balls building as she took the hand from her mouth and moved it to the base of me, cupping my balls, rolling them with her hand. Exploring my body. I was hers to study, in depth, for as long as she wanted. Nothing was capable of moving me from this spot. From her.

"I've never—" Her gaze dropped to the head of my cock. "I've watched stuff, but I—I don't know what I'm doing."

"Lexi." Her name was more moan than word as I buried my hand in the thick masses of her hair. "There is no right or wrong. Take me into your mouth. Use your other hand, wrap it around my cock to control how deep I go. Do whatever you want. Just don't bite."

She pressed one hand into my chest and I stepped back. Slowly, she slid from the settee to her knees before me. Through fringed lashes and with my cock bobbing just in front of her mouth, she looked up at me, holding my gaze as her hand tightened around my cock, about halfway down the long shaft, and opened her mouth.

"Holy fuck."

I closed my eyes as the wet heat of her enveloped me. I vowed not to rush her, but my hand fisted in her silky hair and a growl filled the small room as she worked me with her tongue.

As a cock-sucking virgin, she should have been hesitant. Not my mate. She fucked me with her mouth, taking me deeper and deeper with each movement. I tried to make it last, tried to control my body, but she was too much. I couldn't hold back, not this time, not seeing her for the first time on her knees before me, her mouth stretched wide like I imagined, my cock disappearing into her hot depths. My body was easily giving in to anything my mate demanded.

And right now, she demanded my seed. My pleasure. My surrender. She was ruthless and I loved it.

I gave her everything with a loud cry as she sucked me so hard her cheeks went hollow. As my cock bucked in her mouth, she massaged my balls, stroking and working me, drawing out my orgasm just as I had controlled hers.

When it was over, she leaned back slowly, licking me clean like I was her favorite treat. "That was fun." She raked my thighs with her fingernails and I shuddered.

Gods, I was in trouble here. Until this moment, I'd firmly believed I was in control. Now I knew my folly. Lexi was everything. I could deny her nothing.

"Up, mate. It's time for your reward."

Eager this time, she took my offered hand and stood before me. I wanted more this time. I wanted to see all of her.

"Eager?"

She nodded and bit her lip. "I had no idea it would be like this, that I would feel this...naughty."

"I like a naughty mate. Now take off your dress. I want to look at you."

She hesitated for a moment, but I was before her with my cock hanging naked from my pants, slick from her attentions, with every ounce of desire for her blazing from my eyes. She pulled the dark red fabric off over her head before dropping it to a pool on the floor. She lifted her hands to cover her breasts, but I leaned over her, pulling them away, holding them out to the side as I inspected the luscious curves of my mate.

"You're perfect. So fucking perfect."

Lowering my head, I took first one nipple, then the other into my mouth. She stepped back on shaky legs until her ass bumped into the edge of the settee. It offered her the support she needed as I sampled her lush breasts. I took my time, tasting the soft underside of each one, working my way down over her supple stomach to her hips, her thighs. When I released her arms, she kept them where they were, out to her sides, gripping the edge of the furniture.

Gods, I couldn't wait to fuck her sweet pussy, fill her with my seed. Make her mine forever.

But not tonight. Not yet. I hadn't earned that yet.

It was my turn to kneel once again.

I put my hands to good use, spreading her pussy lips wide for my tongue. I showed her no mercy, tasting and licking, claiming her thoroughly as her pussy clamped down on my finger or my tongue, I made her come over and over until her voice was hoarse from saying my name and her body trembled, too weak to stand.

When she was wrung out and limp, when I knew she couldn't give me anything more, I wrapped my body around her and pulled her into my arms on the long lounge chair, holding her as our breathing returned to normal.

Gods, if it was possible, I fell in love with her then, with the gentle and contented sigh that left her throat as she snuggled into my side. My body melted like a fool's when she draped both an arm and leg over me, linking us as one and claiming me for her own. At least for now.

I wanted forever. One taste and I already knew I could never let her go.

It took time for us to recover. She'd taken my legs out from beneath me better than any Hive fight. When we were both ready, and her eyelids grew heavy, I tucked my cock back into my pants, dressed her gently, and carried her back to her suite.

I wanted to hold her all night. I wanted to take her to my rooms and never let her out of them. But I could not. If she slept naked beside me, I would not be able to resist temptation. I would seduce her and she would let me. Every soft sigh and trusting response of her body told me she would allow me my pleasure.

But I would not betray that trust by claiming her before she was truly ready. When I took her virginity, when I filled her with my seed, I wanted her to be absolutely sure. I wanted her to be in love with me.

I carried her to her suite, set her on her feet and kissed her with as much tenderness as I could muster. When she wrapped her arms around me and kissed me back, pushed her eager tongue into my mouth and invited me to conquer, I obliged, leaving her breathless and needy when I walked away.

No. I wouldn't be the only one aching and desperate until we saw each other again.

exi

"YOU ARE PLAYING WITH YOUR FOOD." DANI GRINNED AT ME, and the knowing look behind her eyes made me blush. "What's the matter? Did having too many orgasms last night ruin your appetite?"

"Dani!" Heat flooded my face and I titled my head, giving her the evil eye where she sat across from me at the small table. The square table had four chairs around it, just like a diner back home, but only three of the seats were taken.

"Don't try to deny it, Lex. We both saw you when he brought you home last night." Katie sipped at a glass of some strange green fruit juice that taste like a bizarre cross between bananas and watermelon. Good, but weird. "And he's already giving you jewelry." Katie deliberately dropped her gaze to the crystal shard around my neck. Bryn, Von's friend, and it seemed Katie's mate—that was a whole other story—had delivered it to our suite as we were leaving for breakfast. Apparently, he and Von and the rest of them had been called out on some kind of mission or something and would be gone all day. I couldn't see Von until tonight, which made me both disappointed and giddy, because I *would* see him tonight. See him, and let him slide his big cock into my...

"How many orgasms was it, anyway? I need a number, a goal for my mate, if he ever decides to show up." Dani talked with her fork, and several heads turned at the table nearest us, the three Earth girls sitting there all burst into laughter.

"Could you two talk any louder?" Seriously. I was going to strangle them both.

Katie grinned, but shut up. Dani, however, laughed. "We're just jealous. Believe me. I'd love to have a man who could make me look like that much of a hot mess."

I smiled and sipped my own juice. The breakfast food was interesting, but didn't taste like home. There was a strange meat that looked like ham but tasted like chicken. The fluffy white stuff that I assumed was some kind of egg was close, but with an odd tang. And the vegetables had been cut into cubes that looked like potatoes but tasted more like turnips. My culinary mind was at war with both my taste buds and my eyes. I would give just about anything to get into that kitchen and taste everything, every meat and vegetable and spice. I could make something great, I just knew it.

We ate in companionable silence for a few minutes until a shadow fell over my chair.

"Miss Lopez. May I join you?" Cosmo's deep rumble made every hair on my body stand on end but before I could formulate a polite response, he'd already pulled back the empty chair and sat down beside me. "How are you, Alexis? Or should I call you Lexi, like Von does?"

The main area of the restaurant was much brighter and livelier than the private rooms upstairs. If we hadn't been in a room surrounded by a ton of people, I would have been freaking the fuck out. As it was, I placed both hands on my lap and cleared my throat as Dani and Katie both stared at our uninvited guest with round, shocked eyes. "I'm great, thanks. And Miss Lopez is fine."

I didn't want him calling me Lexi. That was for friends. And Von, who said my name like it was candy on his tongue, not poison.

"I hear you and Von had a wonderful time after your meal last night." He leaned forward until his lips were inches away from my ear. He raised his hand to wrap it around my arm, just above my elbow. "Did you enjoy the taste of his cock? Was his tongue on your clit enough to win you over? Or do you require more—" Cosmo's other hand came to rest on my thigh, "—direct stimulation?"

I shot to my feet, twisting my arm out of his grip. "Get away from me. Asshole!"

Cosmo lifted his hands up by his head with his palms open and stood, backing away from me with a mocking bow. "I'll see you again later, Lexi. Make sure to tell Von I said hello."

If I could have started his body on fire with my glare, I would have. What kind of demented game was he playing? And why did I get the feeling it had absolutely nothing to do with me, and everything to do with some past history between Cosmo and my mate?

"What an asshole." Dani's soft voice brought me back to the present and I rubbed at my arm absently. It ached a little, but nothing worth crying over.

Katie grabbed my hand when I sat back down. "I don't think you should tell Von."

That got my attention. "Why not?"

Dani and Katie shared a look and I shoved my plate away as I waited for their answer. I had no appetite now. None.

It was Dani who answered, her small, lithe frame a comedy of tragic proportions when compared with the fire in her eyes. "That guy hates your mate."

"No kidding. Thanks for stating the obvious."

Katie rolled her eyes. "He *wants* Von to fight him. He's been trying to get Von to fight him since the very first moment you two met in the big hall."

That was true.

Dani watched Cosmo's broad back as he retreated from the restaurant, and soon, all three of us inspected his large frame, the blue of his Hunter uniform, the massive expanse of his shoulders. Not that I doubted Von, but…

"They obviously have bad blood between them and he's been trying way too hard to get Von to fight him." Dani tapped her fingernail on the hard exterior of her drinking glass, making a steady *tink, tink, tink*. "I don't think you should give Von a reason to take him up on the offer."

I sighed. "You guys don't think Von would kick his ass?"

Katie covered my hand with her own, her eyes big and round and a little too sad for someone who should have been being courted by her own marked mate. "Be with Von. Accept him as your mate and get the hell out of here. Leave Cosmo and all of his bullshit behind. Why take the chance that Von could get hurt when you don't have to?"

My girls had a point.

———

Lexi

. . .

I STARED AT MY REFLECTION IN THE FULL-LENGTH MIRROR AND almost fainted. That couldn't be me. There was just no way.

My dark hair was pulled up and back in an elaborate coif that had taken the Everian woman more than an hour. My makeup was perfect, done by the same kind old woman who had then helped me into about five layers of slips and silk and a corset that made my already curvy figure nearly obscene.

I looked like an anime character, one of the girls whose boobs were so big she was about to topple out of her dress and over onto the ground. Between my breasts hung a single crystal shard gifted to me earlier by Von. His very serious friend Bryn, had dropped it by our suite early this morning and explained that they'd all been called away on urgent Hunter business, but would be back for the ball tonight.

The ball. That was the first I'd heard of it.

With a happy laugh bubbling up from somewhere deep and precious inside me, somewhere I hadn't felt since I was about six years old, I spun in the gorgeous gown, feeling like a fairy princess. The gown was a golden creation that made me feel like Belle in *Beauty and the Beast.* Covered in sparkling crystals and delicate embroidery, it sparkled when I moved. My shoulders were bare, but narrow sleeves hugged my arms all the way down to my small wrists. The gown hugged my upper body to just below my hips where it flared into a full skirt that fell in a cascade of sparkling color to my ankles. The shoes were padded slippers like I imagined a ballerina might wear, but I was grateful that my feet wouldn't hurt all night.

I looked like a princess. I wanted to dance. With *him.*

My mate.

Just thinking of Von made me shiver and I did not recognize the happy glow in my own eyes. This couldn't be real, could it? After last night, when I'd come so many times, been so wrung out I couldn't even walk, he'd carried me to this very suite, kissed me senseless, and left me to my dreams.

Of course, he'd been in them. But not to push me or try anything new. At least newer than what we'd done in the private dining room. I'd gotten on my knees for him. God, that made me a total slut. So did being eaten out in a restaurant. I grinned. Yeah, being a slut with Von was okay by me.

But when he'd come to me in my dream, it hadn't been so frantic, so carnal. He'd wrapped himself around me, holding me all night long. We'd talked about a lot of things. My parents. Their deaths. Leaving culinary school. No money and no life plans. Why I'd stayed a virgin.

Von had told me about the Hive wars, the Prillon battleships and the scary creatures he'd had to kill. They sounded like some nightmare out of a *Star Trek* movie, and his eyes had changed when he talked about the war. And all the killing. I'd thought a bunch of bullying cheerleaders was bad. He'd had evil cyborgs to kill…or be killed.

When even my mind was too exhausted to talk, he'd simply held me like I was the most precious thing in the universe. I'd never felt safer. More cherished.

Loved. I'd felt loved.

Which was completely insane, because I hadn't even known the man a day. Half of that I'd been asleep and he'd been working. The rest of the time he'd had his head between my legs making me chant his name like he was some kind of pagan god.

Maybe he was. My new god. "The god of orgasms."

I laughed at my own joke and twirled once more, watching the skirt shimmer and dazzle in the light.

"What did you just say?" Katie walked into my bedroom in her own gown, a deep blue that brought out the color of her eyes to perfection. Her hair was not up, like mine, but partially so, with the long fall of dark brown tumbling in thick waves down her back.

Caught, I lifted my hand to my lips and pretended to cough. Hell. How was I supposed to cover that one up?

"She said, the god of orgasms." Dani walked in, her fair skin and pale blonde hair glowing like fire above her fitted black gown. She was so small, like a doll. Several inches shorter than me, she looked delicate and brittle, like a prima ballerina, so small I imagined her mate would be able to toss her into the air like a feather. "Mated to the god of orgasms. Lucky bitch."

I curbed my enthusiasm for Von, remembering I wasn't the only one here because of the Brides Program. My heart sank as I watched her sit on the edge of my bed. "I'm sorry I didn't ask you earlier. No luck?"

She sighed and picked at her skirt so she wouldn't have to look at me. "No. He didn't come. I keep dreaming about him, but nope. He's not here."

Katie sat next to her, shoulder to shoulder in a show of womanly support. "Did he say, in his dreams, when he would get here?"

"No." Dani sighed. "I'm not sure he's coming at all."

"What?" I rushed to her, kneeling on the floor in front of her as Katie wrapped an arm around her from behind. I couldn't image dreaming about Von, and never meeting him in the flesh. And now that I knew what it felt like to be held in his arms, to feel his lips on mine, to feel his cock swell and release in my mouth, even more, the bliss of his mouth on me, the horror of not meeting him was all the more real.

"He'll come. Believe me. If he's anything like Von, he'll move heaven and Earth to get to you."

Dani shook her head and stood, shaking off both me and Katie, and our offers of comfort. "That's just it, isn't it? We aren't on Earth anymore."

Katie looked at me and shrugged. There was nothing we could do to help. It wasn't like we could go track down her mate and force him to come claim her. The area of proximity didn't guarantee the guy *wanted* his mate, only that they were close enough to each other to share their dreams.

Katie clenched her hands in front of her waist. "You could always choose someone else. There are a lot of men here. Hot ones."

Dani raised a brow. "Is that what you are going to do, Katie? Choose someone else?"

She shrugged and I didn't like the pain I saw in her eyes, the doubt. "I don't know."

It was my turn to gasp. "What? Why? What happened? I thought you and Bryn were dream sharing." I felt bad, being so focused on Von we hadn't had time to talk.

Katie looked away. "We were."

"But?" I asked.

"But he's an asshole." Katie rose and shook out her skirts. "I don't know about him, Lexi. There's something he's not telling me. And he's acting like a real jerk."

Dani snorted. "Maybe, but you looked a little worse for wear last night when he brought you home. You were about as messed up as Lexi here with her *'god of orgasms'.*"

Before Katie could reply, a knock sounded on the door to our suite and my heart leapt into my throat. Von was here. And tonight, god, tonight he said he was going to take my second virginity.

While I hadn't been with him all day, I'd avoided

thinking about the whole *three virginities* thing. I'd been a complete hussy and sucked his cock. Something I never would have had done with the guys that hadn't interested me on Earth. That had been an easy thing to do. I'd wanted it. Sure, I'd gagged a little because his cock was so dang big, but I'd liked the feel of him in my mouth. I'd liked looking up at him and watching him lose control.

But my ass? I'd never even considered anal sex before. Not even anal play. Butt plugs? Nope. Nothing back there at all.

Tonight, though, he'd take me there. As the crude guys used to say, he'd take that cherry. Was the ball a form of foreplay for all the couples who'd been matched at the event the day before? Were the males just working it so we'd give it up?

I pursed my lips, realized I might just do that. What Von and I had done the night before had been incredible. It hadn't even been scary. Why should I doubt Von? He wouldn't hurt me. He'd said he'd only give me pleasure. If he promised to bring me pleasure by fucking my ass, then I wanted to try it. With him. Only with him.

Taking a deep breath, I realized he was going to slide that hard cock into my tight little bottom. But that wasn't all. No. He said he would fill me front and back, and make me scream for him. Front and back?

My pussy clenched beneath my yards of ball gown and my hand lifted to cover my heart, which was racing like a gelding at the Kentucky Derby.

I wanted that. I wanted everything.

I wanted *him*.

Katie, Dani and I all looked at each other, bracing ourselves for what was to come. Katie giggled first. "It's just like prom night, only this time, we're actually going to have sex after."

Dani rolled her eyes. "Some of us, maybe. Lucky bitches. I'll have to watch your men lead you away, know you get to have a hot, hunk-a man-meat working you over until you can't breathe."

I took her hand and squeezed. "He'll come for you, Dani. Have a little faith."

"I'm all out of faith. Especially when it comes to men." She plucked at an invisible piece of lint on the skirt of her dress and I bit my lip when I noticed her small hand shaking. "So much for the wonderful Interstellar Brides Program. I'm so fucked up not even an alien can deal with me."

"Me, too, Dani. It's not just you." Katie rested her hand on Dani's shoulder briefly before heading to answer the door. There was more to Katie's story, but she wouldn't be sharing now.

I followed her to the living room. When the door opened, my heart stuttered and restarted in my chest. Selfish as it was, I shoved Dani's and Katie's issues away for the night. I wanted to focus on finding my own way tonight. I had faith that things would work out for all of us. I had to. Otherwise, traveling seven light years across the galaxy to another planet was freaking crazy.

And I didn't want to be crazy. I wanted to be happy and loved. I wanted to feel like I finally belonged somewhere, like I had a home. I wanted my mate.

Von.

My mate stood grinning at me from the corridor and I didn't have the good sense to invite him in. Holy crap. He was sex on a stick. My entire body flooded with desire and I couldn't breathe. All I could think about was his mouth on me, his fingers making me come. The taste of him. Watching him lose control. How was I supposed to remember to be polite?

He wore a uniform very similar to the one he'd worn last night, but his boots were polished until they gleamed and his standard brown jacket had been replaced by jet black. His pants and shirt, a tan color the day before, were black as well. He still wore the insignia on his collar, the bars on his arm, the wicked-looking ion blaster strapped to his thigh. He looked dangerous, and so sexy I couldn't tear my gaze from his.

His vivid blue eyes found mine at once and I shuddered as he took his time looking me over from head to toe.

"Lexi."

"Von."

He held out his hand and I walked to him eagerly, his companion and my roommates fading from my awareness like they were part of a dream and I was only now coming awake. Von was so real, so vivid in my mind that I didn't have enough energy left over to keep track of anyone else. He was here. He was my everything.

God, I was obsessed.

I placed my hand in his and he smiled, bending low to kiss the bend of my wrist. Still bent over my hand, he raised his gaze to mine. "I do love to hear you say my name."

I knew I must have blushed a bright red, remembering all the times I'd cried it out in pleasure the night before, but he only chuckled and pulled me to his side, tucking my hand in the crook of his arm as he led me down the hallway to the ballroom.

on

I'D WITNESSED THE TRADITIONAL MATING BALL SEVERAL TIMES over the last few months, always patrolling from the walls or outside, watching decorated Hunters bow and scrape and generally act like idiots to please their women.

Every time, Bryn and I scoffed when it was over, drunk ourselves into a stupor to ignore the lonely ache in our own chests and blathered on about what fools those Hunters be.

And look at us now.

Bryn wandered the edge of the room, clearly hunting for a woman. Katie, I was sure. I wondered what was between them, but he'd been even less talkative than usual, so I hadn't pressed the issue. If he didn't get things resolved before it was time to head back to our mountain fortress, Feris 5, I would need to intervene.

As it was, I had my hands full with my own beautiful

bride. Her black hair was draped atop her head in a style that showed her long neck and ample curves to perfection. Her gown was a pale gold, the color glowing softly against her creamy skin. Her shoulders were bare, the dress clinging to every curved inch of her perfect body. A body I hungered to possess completely.

Unclaimed males hovered around the edges of the dance floor, watching and assessing the connection between mates. Not all matches were marked, and one wrong move from a male, should he anger or disappoint his potential bride, there were others waiting and watching for an opportunity to swoop in and steal the woman's affections.

I pulled Lexi close and wrapped my arm around her as we danced. No one would get near her. She would want no other. I made sure of that, wringing pleasure from her body like a man possessed.

In fact, I was. Nothing made my cock harder than hearing her lust-filled cries, her loss of control, a gift she gave to me. Only to me.

"You are beautiful, mate."

Her cheeks blushed pink and I held her gaze, willed her to see and understand my commitment to her, to us.

"Thank you. You're not so bad yourself."

I looked as I always did, my uniform dress black instead of work brown. "I am nothing special, Lexi. And without you, I am nothing."

"You are so dramatic." Lexi's dark eyes softened at my words and she melted into me as I swirled her slowly around the dance floor. "So, I guess you better keep me around."

"I intend to stay by your side forever." I lowered my head and brushed my lips along her cheek. "Even if I have to beg for the right."

Lexi lifted her arms to wrap both around my neck in a

strange but not unwelcome movement. This new position pushed the tops of her ripe breasts up and placed them on display. Her delicate fingers twined together in my hair, tugging gently and my entire body went on high alert at the subtle, very feminine claim. "You can't be real." Her gaze dropped from mine and scanned the elaborate decorations, the beautiful gowns on the other women and the dangling lights. "None of this can be real."

Hands on her waist, I lowered my forehead until it touched hers. "That is exactly how I feel about you."

Her soft sigh melted the last bit of tension in my body that remained from the day's mission. We'd been sent on an emergency transport into Sector 17, under Commander Grigg Zakar, where the mates and children of several Prillon warriors had been taken captive by Hive Scouts aboard a civilian transport vessel.

They couldn't send in the Atlans, the beasts were too volatile for such a mission. And the nearest human recon team was busy on another op. There had been no time to waste, and no better Hunters to send to retrieve them.

I was the best. Me. Bryn. Our team. We were fast, efficient and deadly. Hive rescue missions had become something of a specialty and we all welcomed the challenge. Keeping the peace and hunting down petty criminals on Everis kept us from death by boredom, but was not enough to satisfy our Hunter blood. We were Hunters. We needed to hunt.

I had served my time in the war, was officially no longer a member of the Coalition Fleet, but I was a Hunter first and always. Bryn and the rest of the men who'd served with me all felt the same. When they needed us, we answered the call. No question.

Although, for the first time, I had hated to leave Everis

behind. The adrenaline that spiked in my blood had been unwelcome and tasted shockingly similar to fear.

For the first time on one of these missions I'd had something to lose.

Lexi. With her soft scent and luscious curves, her shy smile and gentle nature. Passionate and trusting, intelligent and kind. She was everything to me now. Risking my life meant something, not because I cared whether I lived or died, but because I cared about leaving her.

The music ended and I took my mate by the hand, gently leading her to a long table set with sweet treats and refreshment. Away from the dance floor, the lights shone a bit more brightly, making every part of her golden dress shimmer and sparkle as if she were a creature of fantasy and magic, not flesh and blood.

By the divine, I could not take my eyes off her.

"I missed you today." Her whispered confession made my heart lurch. Could it be true? Had my absence affected her as it did me?

"I'm sorry, mate. I was called away on an urgent mission. The Coalition Fleet requested a Hunter Unit. They only do so when there is an extreme emergency."

She stopped walking and tugged on my hand to cease my movement as well. She was so small that I could have tossed her aside like a feather. But the slightest touch of her hand stayed me and I knew it would always be this way.

"What did they need you to do?" Worry clouded her gaze and I wanted nothing more than to kiss it away, but I didn't dare. If I took her lips, I would not be able to stop. And I did not want to share her fire with anyone. Her kisses were for me and me alone.

"The Hive boarded a civilian vessel and took the mates

and children of several Prillon warriors captive. They needed a rescue unit."

"But, how is that possible? The Officiates said the Hive hadn't been close to Everis in over a hundred years."

"Don't worry, mate. They were nowhere near. We transported to Sector 17 for the mission."

She blinked more than once as my words sank in. "So, while I was eating breakfast with my friends this morning, you were transporting halfway across the universe and saving a bunch of women and children from the Hive?"

"Yes."

"That's insane." Her gaze darkened and she stepped back, the light directly above her shining down on her hair and shoulders like a golden halo. "Are you hurt? I had no idea. You could have been out there dying, and I had no idea."

"Lexi—"

"No. You shut up right now. I'm mad at you." Her hands shook as she ran them over my body as if inspecting me for injury.

"I am unharmed."

"You better be." Her hands fluttered over my chest and I took the opportunity to capture her wrists and pull her close, but she resisted, her arms straight and locked at the elbows.

"It was nothing." I could not resist inspecting every inch of her skin and admired the long line of her arms, imagined them wrapped— "What is that?"

"What?"

Holding her wrists with one hand, I lifted my fingertips to a mark just above her elbow. A mark that looked like bruises, from a man's hand. With gentle fingers, I traced the faint purple blemish on her flesh. "Lexi? Who did this to you?"

She yanked her hands free and spun away from me. "It's nothing. Let's get some punch or something."

"Punch?" My protective instincts flared to nearly uncontrollable levels. Lexi was mine, and another had dared raise a hand to her.

"You know, something to drink." Head down, she scurried away and I followed.

"Lexi."

She found the beverages and ladled two cups to the brim before sipping at one and handing the other to me. "Let's just enjoy the dance, shall we?"

Gulping down the drink, I emptied my glass and set it aside. Lexi was using hers to hide her face from me, so I gently removed the ornately sculpted glass from her hand and set it aside as well. Fingers beneath her chin, I lifted her face to mine. She was so beautiful, so fucking beautiful. "Lexi, tell me, or I will challenge every Hunter here until I discover the truth on my own."

She rolled her eyes and lifted her hand to wrap her small fingers around my wrist. "It was nothing, Von. Just forget about it, okay?"

"No. You are mine. Mine to protect. Mine to love. Mine, Lexi." I traced her bottom lip with my thumb and thought about what I would do to her later, stretching her virgin ass and filling her with my cock. "You're mine, and later, I'm going to make sure you never forget that fact again."

"God, you are such a caveman."

"I am not from the caves, mate. I am a Hunter. I am not like your Earth males." Lowering my nose to her flesh, I called upon my advanced Hunter senses and drew the essence of her, of the bruised flesh, into my body. The scent was faint, but there, and one I was all too familiar with. "Cosmo."

Lexi's gasp confirmed what my senses told me. I also knew my prey stood on the far end of the room, leaning his shoulder against one of the large pillars as he watched the ball in his sanctioned role as one of the Officiates, and a protector of the females in attendance. All the females, it would seem, except mine.

Turning, I strode toward him without pause as Lexi hurried along behind me.

"Von, wait!"

I ignored her. Cosmo saw me coming and straightened to his full height. He was large and strong, but I did not fear him. In fact, I felt the opposite. I could not wait to get my hands on his flesh. I would make him bleed. I would rip him to shreds and teach him his place. For years, I'd refused his challenges. He was no Hunter, and there was no honor in defeating a weaker opponent. But he'd injured my mate and forced my hand. I would not show him mercy, suspected he wanted none. "I accept your challenge, Cosmo."

Cosmo's smirk confirmed what I already knew, this wasn't about Lexi, this was about the past. About him...and me.

"Tomorrow, Von. Midday."

"Done."

———

Lexi

Cosmo smirked at me as Von gently led me away, all too pleased with the outcome of events.

I should have listened to Dani and Katie. I should have scrubbed at the skin, or gone to their medical station and asked them to use one of those blue healing wands on my arm. But I'd been afraid word would get back to Von if I did.

Not that it mattered now. That jerk Cosmo got exactly what he wanted, my mate agreeing to fight him tomorrow.

"He'll cheat or something, Von. Don't fight him."

Von led me down a long hallway, one I'd not seen before, but I followed willingly. I was worried, but there was nowhere in the universe I'd rather be than with my mate. Von finally stopped walking and lifted his hand to indicate the door before us. "This is my room, Lexi. I want to take you inside, strip you down and make you mine. But as I know you will not let this go, I will speak this once of Cosmo and never again. Do not fear him. He will not defeat me, and he will not cheat. Cosmo is many things, but he is not a cheat. Nor is he a liar. He has been trying to goad me into fighting him for a long time."

"Why?" This whole macho-man thing didn't make any sense.

"He seeks atonement and vengeance."

"For what?"

Von turned and backed me up against the wall. His legs settled in the thick folds of my gown's skirt as he pressed my shoulders to the cold white wall at my back. "I truly do not wish to talk about Cosmo, mate. I want to kiss you and conquer your pussy with my tongue. I want to make you scream my name before I fill your tight virgin ass with my cock."

He had me at *"conquer your pussy with my tongue"*. He would turn me into jelly, wring orgasm after orgasm from my body, drown me in ecstasy until I'd let him do anything he wanted, for I knew he would bring me nothing but pleasure.

Still. I was a virgin. I never thought I'd be psyched about

going anal before I let a man pop my cherry. But with Von, nothing seemed strange or off limits. The idea of him kneeling behind me like a conqueror, filling me with his hard length made me shudder. I wanted him to fill me up. I wanted him to bury himself in my body and lose control of his. I wanted to be every sexual fantasy he'd ever had come to life. Still, I could just hear my mother's screeching as she rolled over in her grave. She'd probably be on the phone with Father Samuel and praying for my damned soul.

Still, I wanted Von. I wanted him in every way I could have him. I was going to experience everything.

I blinked slowly and realized I'd frozen in his arms. Patient as ever, Von stared down at me. "Are you well, Lexi? Are you afraid?"

"No." I shook my head, licked my lips and his attention dropped to my mouth. "I want you. I want to do this."

"Then what is wrong?"

"On Earth, I…It's forbidden. A sin. I shouldn't want you that way."

Von stopped stroking my hair and lowered his lips to mine. One soft, chaste kiss and I nearly swooned. With one finger under my chin, he tilted my face up. No one was about. We were alone in the hallway outside his room. Everyone was either still at the ball or in their rooms getting it on.

His eyes were serious. "From your hesitation, and from what I've heard from other males about their mates from Earth, claiming a mate in the sacred order of the three is not a common occurrence where you are from?"

"I'm a virgin, so I'm not a good guide for what's common. But no. Anal sex is considered a sin by some. Adventurous by others, but definitely naughty."

He arched a brow and the corner of his mouth tipped up.

"So you haven't been saving all three of your virginities simply because you did not meet the right Earth man?"

"No. I never wanted anyone before, not like this." I lifted my hand to his chest and dared a little more, running my palm over his powerful frame until I reached up, twirling my fingers in his dark brown hair. "Before you, I thought—"

His eyes clouded and he lowered his forehead to touch mine as I lifted my other hand to his neck. I loved touching him like this. It made this more real somehow, made him more mine.

"Thought what, Lexi?" he whispered.

"I thought I was broken. I thought something was wrong with me. All my friends were having sex and partying, and I just never...wanted anyone." I lifted my head slightly so I was looking straight into his eyes. "I'd never even considered anal sex before coming here, and back home I probably would've had regular sex before I gave someone a blow job."

"Blow job?"

God, could this conversation get any more embarrassing? "You know, putting my mouth on your cock?" Even though I'd done it the night before, I still blushed.

"But I loved feeling your hot mouth sucking on my cock. As I loved the taste of your pussy coating my lips and tongue."

He said it like it was an absolute fact, like we were discussing the weather. "You make me feel so naughty," I countered, my pulse racing.

"Do you like to be naughty, my Lexi?"

"Yes." Holy hell, yeah, I did. I felt my cheeks heat even more and his smile widened.

"Did you like what we did last night?" His thumb stroked back and forth over my cheek and it was hard to concentrate on what he was saying. Just a simple touch and I was eager for him. Eager for more.

"You know I did," I countered. "I screamed your name loud enough." I grumbled the last and he lifted my chin up a little more, talking to me between kisses.

"Do not be ashamed of what we do. It is perfect. Special. Unique. And if you want to spread your legs nice and wide for me, thrashing about as I lick your perfect pussy, then that's what I'll do."

His words painted a vivid image almost as hot as a caress of his skilled tongue had been on my tender folds.

He grew serious and his teasing kisses stopped. "Have I pleased you, Lexi? Do you dream of another man's hands on your body, his tongue making you cry out?"

Was he out of his mind? I shook my head, but held his gaze. "I don't want anyone else."

His gaze heated. "Good. Your body, your orgasms are just for me. I am a very possessive mate."

"Your body and orgasms are just for me too, then."

"Just for you," he confirmed. "I claimed one of your virginities last night. Did I please you? Are you ready for more?"

His gaze dipped to my mouth and he slid his thumb to run over my bottom lip, then pushed into my mouth. I licked at the tip before sucking on it, just as I had his cock. Yes, he'd definitely claimed my mouth.

"You did a very good job and you know it."

He grinned, forcing a smile from me as I released his thumb. The warmth in his eyes set me at ease, but not completely. I was nervous. I couldn't help it. "I am nervous. I'm trying not to be. But I didn't say I didn't want this." I shook my head. "I said I *shouldn't* want this. But I do. I shouldn't want you to fuck my ass, but I do."

His eyes flared then with heat and he took my hand and led me down the hall once again, this time our pace was a little quicker. I took in his large shoulders, his powerful frame and drop-dead gorgeous face. He was too good to be true, and he was leading me to his room to take my body in a way I'd never dared imagine, let alone want.

But I did now. I wanted whatever he would do to me, knew I would experience nothing but sensual bliss under his touch.

Oh. My. God. Three days ago I was on Earth, a virgin hoping that there was some guy *out there* that *might* be interested in me. Might be interested in making me come, possibly before he did. Might find my curves hot.

And now I was going to have Von's thick cock—and I knew how thick it was because it had been deep down my throat the night before—claim my ass. My ass! I'd never even considered anal sex until the three virginities were explained. I'd been so focused on old-fashioned sex, a man filling my vagina, that I hadn't considered anything else.

I wanted to do this. Perhaps I'd been injected with not just an NPU for language processing, but a slut button and Von had not only found it, he'd pushed it. Hard.

He'd said that besides dream sharing, we'd also become more and more horny for each other as time passed, that the need to claim each other was deeply rooted in our newly awakened marks. He said the desire that flowed between marked mates was fierce and undeniable. I believed him now. I was eager for this. For him. Anything we would do together would be all right as long as he was touching me, making me his.

When the door to his room closed behind us, I looked about. His rooms were similar to the suite I shared with the girls, only smaller. It seemed the men didn't share. This worked for me because while the idea of someone seeing me with Von at the restaurant would have been embarrassing. This? This needed to be done all alone.

"Take off your clothes."

13

SPINNING ON MY PRETTY HEELS, I SAW VON LEANING AGAINST the closed door with his arms crossed. He was watching me with a gaze so heated I was surprised my dress didn't burst into flames.

"Don't you want to help?"

Slowly, he shook his head.

What was it about a man in uniform? So commanding, so bold. I wanted to do just as he said.

"I want to see what's underneath. Our dream sharing only goes so far. I want to see all of you tonight." His gaze drifted over every inch of me, from my toes to the tip of my head. "I want to taste you everywhere, every inch, Lexi."

I shivered. Hell yeah, I wanted that too. I reached behind me, trying to find the buttons of my dress. Frustrated I turned, giving him my back. "I can't get out of the dress alone."

The soft sound of his boots on the thick carpet as he neared had me closing my eyes in anticipation. When his fingertips traced the back of my shoulders and neck before wandering down my spine to the top of the dress, I swayed into him, wanting more than just the small ends of his fingers on my skin.

With deft fingers, he undid the buttons one by one. Once loose, I spun back around, holding the bodice in place.

The top swells of my breasts were exposed little by little as I lowered it. When I saw his eyes watch the motion, I slowed down. My thoughts of being taunted and jeered for my full breasts, ample hips and round butt cooled some of my eagerness. "I'm not...thin."

He smiled. "By the Divine, no you are not."

I wasn't sure what that meant, but he appeared eager to see my body again. Arms crossed, I hoped his reaction was a true one, but years of doubt, of chubby girl taunts on the school bus and the skinny girls giggling and laughing at me in the locker room rose to the fore and I froze.

Von lifted his gaze to mine. "I want to see your soft body, mate. You are beautiful. Show me what's mine." He returned his attention to my chest, just tilted his chin to indicate I should continue, his words slipping through my body like warm caramel heating my blood.

"I'm going to get lost in your breasts. They'll overflow my palms and your nipples will be taut and full in my mouth. When I suck on them, the hard little tips will press against my tongue. Your hips, as you said, are curvy. Perfect for gripping as I fuck you. And your ass?"

He glanced up, his eyes a dark blue. So vivid. So alive. So fucking eager.

"Plump. A perfect cushion for my hips every time I slam into you, my cock buried deep. Tonight, when I take your ass, when I stretch you open so perfectly, I'll watch your flesh quiver and shake as I claim you."

My hands had stopped at his words. Heat pulsed through me in a carnal wave. I'd never thought about my body that way before. Was that how he saw me? For the first time since I was ten and I started to develop, I felt pretty. I felt desired. With renewed eagerness, I let the dress drop from my fingers and onto the floor. Von's quick intake of breath was my reward, his hands actually shook as he lifted them to my face.

"Fuck, Lexi. I should punish you for wearing things beneath your dress, but I'm overwhelmed. No more panties, mate." He lowered his head to steal a kiss and I felt the truth of his desire in the kiss, in the tenderness of his touch. And I felt gorgeous, which was a small miracle all by itself. "My memories of you did not lie. You're gorgeous."

He broke the kiss and stepped back, his gaze roving, taking his time. "I want you, Lexi. You're beautiful, mate. By the Divine, you're perfect."

I didn't look down at myself, but at him watching me. I knew he could see my corset and panties, my heels.

Before I could blink, he'd stripped everything from me, easily forgotten on the floor. He was on me then, lifting me up and carrying me across the room to the bed.

"Von! Put me down. I'm too heavy."

I heard the swat to my bottom a split second before I felt it.

"Do not belittle yourself."

"But—"

"Do you want me to spank you again?"

He tossed me onto the bed and I bounced and came up onto my knees, but he gripped my ankle.

The sting from his palm was minor, but the heat that flared from it made my pussy so wet and achy.

A slow grin spread across his face. "You do."

"I do, what?" I asked, tugging at his hold on my ankle.

"You do want me to spank you again."

"I do not!" I countered, tugging with more effort, which was completely wasted.

"I know you, Alexis Lopez. We've dream shared. You've sucked my cock. I've claimed one of your virginities. You are my marked mate. You can hide nothing from me. Your pulse is racing and your skin is flushed. Your eyes are big and dark with desire. You liked the sting of my hand on your ass."

With a twist of his wrist, he skillfully rolled me onto my stomach. I could do nothing but gasp at the ease with which he maneuvered me.

"You should have told me about Cosmo. You will never keep something like that from me again."

Reaching down, he stroked his palm over the curve of my butt, over the heat where I knew his handprint was. He spanked again, but in a different spot. My muscles tightened instinctively.

"Tell me, Lexi. Promise me. No more secrets. I can't protect you if you lie to me." His hand landed on my ass again and I gasped, my entire bottom on fire. But worse, my pussy throbbed with each beat of my heart, my arousal making the plump lips actually hurt with want.

"Von."

"Promise me." One hand on the curve of my back, he slid the other hand lower and slipped one finger inside my dripping core. I was so tight, and my body clamped down on his finger like a fist making me gasp and squirm, pushing back, trying to get more of him. Yes. I wanted him. Now.

"I promise. I promise."

He massaged my ass with one hand and played with my pussy with the other, spreading my wet welcome all over my pussy lips and ass. "You're so nice and wet. I think you liked your punishment, mate."

I looked over my shoulder at him. His uniform so crisp and commanding. His eyes potent and definitely lethal to any defenses I may have. Hands big and I imagined quite skilled. The outline of a thick, hard cock at the front of his pants.

Oh. My. God. There it was. His big dick. That was going to go in my ass. My mouth watered, remembering the taste of him, the feel of it, silky soft and hard against my tongue. The flared head so wide I had to stretch my lips open. So thick I had to breathe through my nose and swallow to take him deeper.

That was going in my ass.

This wasn't one sided though. He would make sure I came, too. Probably more than once with that skilled tongue of his. I knew he'd make me feel good no matter how naughty the act.

Yes, please.

So I did the only thing a reasonable woman could do in this situation. I licked my lips and demanded he take me.

Von growled. Literally growled. Gripping my hip, he pulled me up and back so I was on my forearms and knees. In seconds he'd knelt by the bed, his mouth clamped down in hard suction on my clit.

"Von!" I cried.

The heat of his tongue was almost scalding as it slid down over my tender skin.

"Wet and delicious. You're going to come on my mouth, then when you're nice and soft, I'll get this all ready for me."

The tip of his finger tapped my virgin hole and I gasped.

"Yes." It was all I could say. What else was there? I wanted to come. I wanted whatever he was going to give me. Since taking all three virginities was an Everian custom, I highly doubted that every couple on the planet would practice anal sex if the women all hated it. There would have been a revolt. Officiate Treva would have warned us just to bear it and deal with how miserable the act made us feel.

But no. She hadn't said that. No one mentioned it was something to endure. It seemed like Von and every mated couple knew something I didn't. Knew how good it could feel. I'd never been with a man, so I had no idea what anything was supposed to feel like. I just knew Von made me feel good, and I trusted him. I wanted him to teach me about sex and love and pleasure. I came across the galaxy to find a man who could make me feel lust and desire like he did. I wasn't going to deny myself a chance at pleasure now.

With his hands on my hips, he held me in place as he ate me out. There was no other way to describe his mouth on my body because he wasn't gentle or the least bit tender about the act. He was a parched man and my pussy juices were bringing him back to life. My clit was so sensitive to him that each press of his tongue made me moan, the suction of his lips made my fists clench in the sheets.

With my ass up, head down, I buried my loud cries in the soft blanket, my fingers gripping it for dear life. I cried out his name again and again as the crest approached, pushing me higher and higher until I felt like I was going to shatter into so many pieces I'd never be put back together again. It was too good and when he sucked and flicked in some special way, I screamed and went stiff as my core went into a massive spasm. I forgot to breathe as the orgasm ripped through me on the inside, leaving nothing but a whimpering and submissive creature behind.

Von made me fall apart, but his hands soothed me,

stroking my back and round ass as he crooned and kissed me, telling me how beautiful I was, how much I meant to him. His touch kept me grounded and I let myself give over to him as the last aftershocks rolled through me. And that was just his mouth. He hadn't fucked me yet, hadn't claimed my ass. I wasn't sure I was going to survive. I'd never felt anything this intense in my life.

I was going to die from pleasure.

"That's a good girl," he murmured when he finally lifted his head, kissing the handprint I knew was on my ass. His lips left a wet spot on my heated flesh, evidence of my arousal.

He moved to the side of the bed, grabbed the bottle of lube on the side table. This was a foregone conclusion, getting me into his bed, ass up. That fact should have bothered me, but it didn't. This was Everis and I wanted Von to take me as he wanted, his way.

"Don't move," he warned.

"You're still dressed," I countered. "I don't think this is going to work very well if *that* is still in your pants."

I wore nothing but my heels, on all fours, ass skyward while he was fully dressed. His mouth and chin were glistening. From me. It was the sexiest moment I'd ever imagined and I felt like the star of a movie, finally the center of someone's world. I finally belonged to someone and he belonged to me.

"You're too much for me, Lexi. If I take my cock out now, I'll shoot my load all over that spanked ass. Do you want my seed marking your ass on the outside or the inside?"

My pussy clenched then at the visual. Knowing I'd made him eager enough to spurt all over me was really hot, but the idea of his cock stretching me open and then burying deep, coating my inner walls with his seed had me whimpering.

"Inside."

He opened the lid on the lube as he came around behind me. I felt the cool liquid dribble down between my ass cheeks and I startled. His finger brushed over my clit, circled the entrance to my pussy.

"The ultimate prize. When you are ready to be mine, completely, I'll take you here." I clenched down, trying to draw that finger into me again, but all he did was brush over the sensitive flesh. "So eager, aren't you? Not yet. Not until you say the words, give me everything."

In this moment, I'd have done almost anything for that finger to slide deep into my pussy and I whimpered. I wanted him to claim me, but I wanted this, too.

"Here first, Lexi." His finger slid through the lube, brushed over my tight hole. "Shh. Just a finger. For now."

He circled and swirled, pressed and retreated. I breathed through it, tried to relax. Play, that was all he was doing. Eager now, I started to wiggle my hips, to enjoy the erotic feelings of his finger playing with my ass. My desire overcame any embarrassment and he worked his way into me.

I flowered open for him, slowly, and I panted, gripped the sheets. The coldness of more lube slid over me, then warmed as he worked the liquid inside, deeper and deeper.

"Another finger."

He was so patient, listening to my body, letting it respond to his entry. With one hand working to prepare my ass, he used the other to stroke my clit slowly, deliberately, just enough to make it impossible to decide which way I needed to push, down toward the bed, and more pressure on my sensitive nub, or back to spread my burning ass open on his fingers. I wanted both.

Von kept me on the edge for long minutes, keeping me

aroused, working me with both hands. "One more," he said, some time later, and he worked a third finger deep into my ass.

By then I was squirming, pushing back so his fingers went deeper. I was trying to fuck his fingers and ride his other hand, rubbing my body back and forth between the two pleasure points.

"Do you want me to fuck you now?" he murmured. Leaning forward, I felt his uniform against my heated skin. His voice fanned my ear.

I nodded into the bed. "Yes."

I did want him to. So badly. My body had spiraled to the brink of a second orgasm, and the naughty slide of his fingers in my ass did something to me I didn't understand. I loved the feeling of him filling me, I loved his fingers on my clit. I loved the fact that I was bent over naked on his bed while he was fully dressed. The whole thing seemed so naughty. Forbidden. And that made me so fucking hot I couldn't think, I just wanted more. I wanted to be bad. Really bad. I wanted to try everything, every dirty, taboo, forbidden thing I'd ever heard or read about…with him. Only with him.

God, who knew I was such a naughty, naughty girl?

His fingers slid into me, then retreated, mimicking what his cock would be doing soon enough. I felt more lube, his entry and retreat slick and easy. No pain. An odd feeling of being open, but it was so good. I had no idea there were so many nerve endings, so much pleasure…*there.*

All at once he slid from me and I heard him rip off his clothes. I didn't move. I didn't want to. I knew he could see everything, my pussy swollen from the orgasm he'd wrung from me, my arousal dripping down my thighs, my asshole all prepared and slick with lube, my breasts dangling in front of me. The heels.

By remaining still, I was presenting myself to him, offering him the next part of me. On Earth, it was a sign of deep trust and of submission, complete surrender. Here, it was no different. I trusted Von to make both of us feel good, to take us a step further in our mating process, to bond us even closer.

I felt the bed dip behind me and I startled when his hand slid down my back.

"Shh," he soothed. "You are so beautiful. So mine. You might think of this as *me* taking your ass, mate. This is not the case. This is not what an Everian male sees in this moment."

I stilled at his words. Confused.

"I see you, perfectly ready, positioned perfectly for you to *give* yourself to me. You are giving me your perfect body, your heart, everything that is you. I'm not taking your body, I am humbly accepting everything you offer. It is a privilege to have a mate present herself like this, to accept this gift."

I sighed then, my body relaxing even further. I'd had no idea that I'd still been tense, but his words changed my perspective. What we were doing was special. A bond I'd never have with anyone else. I *was* giving myself to Von. An offering of my body to make our bond stronger and he wasn't devaluing that. He wasn't making this into some kind of cheap porno where he fulfilled one of his sex fantasies. This wasn't Earth.

This was Everis and my ass, it was a gift. And I was giving it freely.

"I want you," I murmured, waiting.

His hand settled on my hip, his thumb tugging on one cheek of my bottom to open me up. I sensed a carefulness to Von. While his touch was deliberate, it also held a level of reverence. The head of his cock was slick and firm as it pressed at my tightly furled rosette.

"Breathe, Lexi. Exhale, yes. Again. Good. Now every time you exhale, push back and take me inside." I did as he instructed and he moaned, encouraging me. "Yes, like that."

I couldn't help but wince as my tissues began to stretch, felt the slight burn at him trying to gain entry. He'd prepared me well though, opening me and coating me liberally in lube. It didn't take long for him to press forward with a pop and he settled just inside.

I groaned and gripped the blanket. "Oh my god," I murmured. Holy cow. It was...big. God, his cock felt huge! Somehow, *there*, everything seemed more intense, and he wasn't doing anything, just giving me a minute to adjust.

He slipped his fingers around to find my clit. My mind veered from the awkward feel of him breaching me to pleasure. Somehow the slight pain from his entry morphed into a swirl of heat. Nerve endings I didn't know existed flared to life and I cried out. This wasn't the usual feel of arousal. It was different but no less intense.

"Nice and slow, mate," Von said, pushing into me an inch or so. It felt like more, but everything he was doing was *more*. He pulled back and I cried out.

Between his fingers plucking and playing with my clit and his in-and-out motions of his cock, my body was riding the razor's edge. If he would just fuck me, take me, ride me...

The images built in my mind and I squeezed down on his cock, making him growl. I did it again and moved my hips back, pushing him deeper. God. Yes. He was so huge. I was so full, so stretched, so fucking dirty. He was rubbing my clit hard, over and over. I was going to come.

He froze, his finger stopped. "Not yet. Do not come until I tell you."

I couldn't believe Von was telling me I couldn't come. I hadn't expected even to like it, let alone be able to come so quickly. It was like he'd lit a match on a fuse, a very short one, and I was going to explode.

"Von, please!" I begged.

God, I was pleading with him for more. Harder. Deeper. Faster. I didn't care if it hurt a little. I didn't care, I simply *needed*.

"Not yet."

His patience waned a bit and I couldn't stop moving. I was mindless now, my body taking over. I pushed my hips back to take more of him as he worked himself in and out. Deeper and deeper until I felt his hips pressing against my stinging bottom.

He was all the way in and he was huge. The walls of my pussy were being stretched from behind, the emptiness there making me mewl like a frustrated kitten. I moved my own hand to my clit and started to rub my sensitive nub hard and fast. My ass clenched down on him and my other fist was white-knuckled in the blanket. I felt like a bomb, the pressure inside me too much to contain. I needed release. I couldn't take this anymore. I couldn't.

"It's too much. I need to come!" I wailed.

His free hand came down on my ass in a gentle spank, making me clench about him as the heat spread like an electric jolt to my system, making me want to come all the more. He used his own hand to still mine.

"When I say, mate."

I whimpered in reply.

He began to move in earnest then. Smooth strokes, almost all the way out and then sliding deep to press against my bottom again and again.

My head thrashed on the bed, my fingers cramped at

how tightly I gripped. His fingers covered mine where I touched myself, guiding the pace. He didn't stop their skilled assault on my clit. I was lost in my submission to him. He controlled everything, my body. My hand. My mind. I was beyond rational thought, lost in this moment, in him.

His hand squeezed on my hip just before he thrust deep, the sound of our flesh slapping together filled the room. "Now, Lexi. Now. We'll come together."

I'd been on the brink, just waiting for his command. I didn't have to do anything but let go, but I knew when I fell, he'd catch me. His shout of release echoed in the room as I felt hot jets of his seed filling me, coating me. Marking me.

His cock swelled, the extra girth making me burn anew as he lost himself in my body, in the pleasure I knew only I could give him. My mark burned on my chest, the heat spreading through me like lava as I exploded beneath him.

I clenched and squeezed, milked his cock with my ass as I came. My pussy was lonely, but somehow the combination of him playing with my clit, an empty pussy and a full ass made it all so much more erotic. Made me crave the final step of our joining.

My entire body went rigid beneath him and I lost all thought and control, collapsing on the bed with him lying on top of me, his cock still buried deep.

When the fire raging in my blood cooled enough that I could catch my breath and get my bearings, I realized he was holding most of his weight off me with his arms, his nose buried in my hair as he nuzzled me. I was a melted puddle in his embrace, unable and unwilling to move. I wanted his skin touching mine. I wanted this. Him.

"You're mine, Lexi. Mine." His hot breath penetrated the thick fall of my hair where it had come undone from its pins and I had to shake my head a bit so I could turn to face him over my shoulder.

"And you're mine," I replied right back, slumping down on the cool bedding as he carefully pulled out, his sign of possession slipping from me to run down my thighs.

14

I loved seeing my Lexi this way. Flushed and relaxed, a smile curving her lips. I kept one arm about her waist, for her legs were wobbly. After I'd claimed her ass, I'd retrieved a warm cloth and cleaned her. I didn't tell her that the sight of my cum slipping from her was one of the most erotic things I'd ever seen. The way she'd given herself to me had been...it was indescribable. The level of trust she had in me was more than I ever expected from another.

Even now, walking her back to the suite of rooms she shared, my mouth watered, remembering the taste of her sweet pussy. I was hooked on her, the addiction stronger than to an illicit drug from Xalia. I would never get enough of her lush body, the way she trembled and quivered just before she came, her soft whimpers and her lusty screams, her taste, her scent. Everything.

Gods, every new thing we did together was hotter than

the last. I'd thought it had been incredible seeing her mouth opened wide for my cock, the feel of her throat as she swallowed me down. Then I'd thought it was the sight of her presenting herself for the second claiming. Then the sight of my cock disappearing into her virgin hole. The sound of her little pants of pleasure as she accepted me. The way she'd begged to come was a definite balm to a Hunter's tender ego. I'd expected her to love it, but she was from Earth and I was concerned it might be too much for her. It seemed the Everis genes were strong with her as she loved the connection between us as much as I. The cry of her orgasm as she clenched down on my cock, pulling me in deeper, finished me off. No Everian, no matter how brave, strong or powerful could hold back their release.

Would it ever stop, this need I had for her?

I doubted it. I didn't want it *ever* to stop.

She'd practically unmanned me, stripping away all my senses, my ability to listen for danger, even to remember that I was a Senior Hunter. I couldn't have claimed her second virginity anywhere else but my private rooms. I couldn't leave her vulnerable to bastards like Cosmo when she weakened my defenses so completely.

"Are you sore?"

I saw her cheeks flush a bright pink at my question and I imagined she'd have to be a little uncomfortable. Everian females were raised knowing the three virginities practice and in most cases, waited for their mate to claim them. Yes, there were widows or those who did not wish to abstain for their marked mate. I couldn't blame them, I hadn't. But anal sex wasn't considered dirty on Everis as it seemed Lexi made it out to be. What we'd done was not shameful and I would teach her that. What we'd done together was perfect. She was perfect.

"A little," she admitted.

"Then I will wait to take you there again. You liked it, did you not?"

The corner of her mouth tipped up. "You know I did. I had no idea I was so noisy when I came."

I grinned then. My male ego preened, knowing I'd satisfied her so thoroughly.

"It's a good thing, then, that you have one virginity to go." The idea of sinking into her pussy made my cock rock hard. Again. This time, when I marked her with my seed, it might take root, make a baby. The ultimate claiming. Then she would be mine and there was no way she could be taken from me. She could not claim another.

I considered her mine now, rules be damned, but taking her pussy, filling her with cum would legally bind us as one, but taking her as our marks touched would seal our mating bond, the mystical connection shared by marked mates.

"Tomorrow, after the challenge. I will take that pussy that is always so eager and wet for me. Yes?" I asked.

"Do you really have to fight Major Cosmo?" Her soft voice was raspy from her screams of pleasure.

I only wanted to hear her say "yes". Instead, she asked about Cosmo. With a sigh, I answered.

"I do. I can't refuse the challenge, nor do I want to. He *touched* you, Lexi. Marked your delicate skin."

The thought of Cosmo putting his hands on her had me seeing red and wanting to track him down and beat him bloody. I was justified and anyone else who was two-thirds through their marked mate's claiming would agree with me. Everyone but Cosmo. We'd been like brothers once. But that made his insult all the worse.

No one touched my mate.

A Junior Hunter walked toward us and saluted. I offered

him a nod in response before continuing on. It reminded me we were not alone in the public hallway.

"What's the deal with you two? Why do you hate him so much?" she asked.

I shrugged, knowing my vague response when she wanted answers the night before would not hold now. Not now that I'd challenged him. I wanted to take her somewhere private to explain, but if we went back to my room, there would be no talking. Only wild fucking. Her suite was off-limits to males. While I wasn't pleased with the rule since I hated anything that kept her from me, I was content knowing no other male would gain entry either. Especially Cosmo.

"We are of similar age, raised in the same region. Our fathers were friends. We grew up as brothers, close friends from the time we were small."

"So what happened?"

"What often does. A woman."

My mate frowned at that and stepped away from me, a move I did not care for. "Did you love her?"

I smiled, lifting my hand to cup her cheek. "No, mate. She was ambitious and wild. A Hunter's abilities do not reveal themselves until he reaches a certain age. She had chosen Cosmo, seduced him, promised her love to him. He fell in love with her, but when we came of age…" I faltered, my mind wandering back to the day I'd found her naked in my bed. The day she'd cursed me to years of guilt and cost me a friend.

"You were a Hunter and he wasn't?"

"We are both Hunters, but not all of us are born with the same level of skill." Narrowing my focus, I allowed my gaze to wander over the perfection of her features, the darkly arched brows, the full lips, her warm, compassionate eyes.

"Cosmo is a Hunter by birth, but the gifts were not as strong with him. He was not assigned to the elite units. She was hungry for status and when she discovered the truth—"

"She dumped him and tried to seduce you instead."

I chuckled. "Do all Earth women finish a man's sentences?"

That made her laugh. "Only the good ones."

I traced her lower lip with my thumb. "Then you must be a very good mate."

"I try." She kissed the tip of my thumb but turned her head away to resume our walk down the hall as I fell into step beside her, where I would always be. "So, that's it? Was he really that stupid? Didn't he know what she was doing?"

"Of course. But the heart and the mind do not always have kind words for one another."

"So, he couldn't let it go."

"No, he could not."

"So you have to fight him now because of some stupid girl from your childhood?" She seemed angry at Cosmo and that pleased me. Thank the Divine any interest he had for her was not reciprocated. "This is like high school all over again. It's ridiculous."

"I don't disagree. Which is the reason I have never accepted a challenge from him before."

"He doesn't seem stupid, Von. Why would he keep this up for so long over a girl who didn't even love him?"

I shrugged. "Over the years, his hurt turned bitter and cold. He believes things come too easy for me. My rank, my hunting skills. And now you, a marked mate, something so rare most of us never dare dream to find it."

"You didn't win me in a battle. We were marked to be together since birth." Yes, she was right about our marks and I was thrilled to know she believed that. "And he's a major.

He's still a Hunter. It's not like he went off to live in a hole and never recovered."

"A major, while high ranking, is not as respected or revered as an elite Hunter."

"And you are a Senior Hunter, which makes you what? The best of the best?"

I only shrugged, for while I was skilled at hunting, I was not invincible, nor was I without flaws, such as jealousy, possessiveness, and obsession for my new mate.

"Then why fight him now? Just walk away, like before."

I took a step back, stopping to straighten my shoulders. "Not this time. He made it personal. He touched you. This is about honor, Lexi. Your honor. When he touched you, he knew I could not allow the assault to go unchallenged."

"He's an idiot. Seriously. Like a five-year-old holding a grudge." She shook her head and reached for my hand, squeezed. "And I don't want you to get hurt."

"If that is your concern, I am not the one you should worry about," I said, my voice low. Cosmo was going down. While I wouldn't kill him, I could certainly put him in a position never to challenge me again. He hadn't hurt Lexi, just used her to get what he wanted...his chance to strike at me, to salvage his own wounded pride.

"Why didn't he just leave me alone?"

"There is one thing you are forgetting...your beauty. You are desirable to more males than just me. Perhaps he hopes if he can dishonor me tomorrow, you will turn from me, reject me, just as the woman he loved rejected him." The last I grumbled and my arm tightened about her, making her look up at me.

Her flushed cheeks and her bright eyes were almost my undoing. There was an emotion that I'd not seen before, soft and warm and something I didn't dare name. Not yet. Not until she spoke the words. "That's so not going to happen. I want you, Von. I just don't want you to fight this stupid challenge."

"Perhaps he would concede the challenge if you were already claimed."

"Meaning you take all my virginities," she clarified.

"Yes."

"Then do it."

I leaned down so I was eye level with her. "What are you saying?"

She licked her lips, looked away, then back. "I don't want Cosmo to win me."

My eyes narrowed at the idea. "He will not win. You do not need to worry about this. He's just an inconvenience. Even if he did win—" Those words were like acid in my mouth. "You make the ultimate choice in your mate. While I have claimed two of your virginities, you can walk away now if you desire. Only when I have taken you completely will we be legally mated. Only then you will be truly mine. Forever."

"Then do it now. I want it. I want *you*."

My cock pressed against my pants, agreeing with her. My mind, though, was still in charge.

"I will not claim you because you do not wish me to fight. I don't want you to be mine out of fear. You will be mine because we were destined, fated, to be together, because you want me and accept my protection." I kissed her hard and fast on the mouth. "I will claim you when you beg me to fill you, when you are as obsessed with me as I am with you, when you surrender to the bond between us and fall in love with me."

Her eyes were round with surprise at my ranting, but I couldn't seem to stop.

"I want everything, Lexi. I won't settle for less."

"All right." Her words left a tight ache in my chest but I brushed it aside. She was young and innocent, naïve and beautiful. She would need time to process my words, time for love to grow. And I was a Hunter. I could be patient, give her the time she needed to settle things in her own mind.

"You never answered my earlier question. Tomorrow, Lexi? Are you ready to be mine?" I was patient, but I wasn't a fool. I could take a lifetime earning her love, but I wanted her firmly under my protection, my bonded mate so I could take her home and get her settled into a new life on the mountain, a life with me. No more empty bed. No more dark, sleepless nights spent staring at the ceiling alone. She was mine and I was hers, and I wanted to take her home as quickly as possible.

She tilted her head up and I saw the smile, the eagerness. "Yes. I… I want to be yours. And I want to come tomorrow. I want to be there when you defeat Cosmo."

I stood to full height. "Absolutely not."

She frowned, a little V forming in her brow. "Why not? It's my fault. If it weren't for me, you wouldn't be fighting him at all. I should be there. I want to be there, for you."

"Your fault?" What the hell was she talking about? "It's not your fault. Cosmo is just being an ass and making my life hell. Our animosity goes back years, way before you even were old enough to be matched through the Brides Program. This isn't about you, it's about him trying to fuck with me and it's high time I ended it."

"Still," she replied. "I need to know you are safe. I want to be there."

"I assure you no harm will come to me. I am a trained fighter and Cosmo is no competition. You do not need to leave your suite to know this fact."

She crossed her arms over her lovely chest. "My suite?"

"Yes, where you will be for the challenge so I will know you are safe."

"I can be safe from the sidelines."

It was my turn to frown. "I do not know what sidelines are, but you are my mate and you must be where I know no harm will come to you. It is for your protection. I will not have any male touching you, Lexi."

"I'm not a child," she countered.

I looked down her body, took in her lush curves, remembered the way she'd had her ass thrust up in the air for me to claim it. "I am well aware of that."

That made my cock thicken impossibly farther and so I took her arm and continued toward her suite. At the door, I cupped her jaw. "Tomorrow, after the challenge, I will come for you. Be ready, Lexi, for I am most eager now. I will come for you, mate. Be ready."

I thought of her beneath me, thighs spread and pussy dripping. Taking her at first gently, and then releasing the pent-up battle rage as well as my cum deep inside her, at the opening of her womb. Making her mine forever. Perhaps giving her a child.

"Good night, Von," she said, the words a little clipped.

I knew she was disappointed, but her slight upset was a small price to pay to ensure her safety. Her protection was my top priority.

I couldn't kiss away her hurt, for if I took her mouth and she opened herself to me, I wasn't sure I had the will to tear myself away. I'd taken two virginities and my body was pushing me to make her mine completely. With a growl, I walked away, knowing the only thing keeping me from claiming her pussy was my honor.

15

——————

I KNEW IT WAS A DREAM, BUT IT SEEMED SO REAL. I COULD FEEL the heat of large machines on my face, smell the sweat from Von and the other Hunters. We were in some kind of engine room, but I'd never been in one before. I'd never been in dreams with Von before either. In these, I somehow knew details, perhaps because of the sharing. We were on a space ship, not Everis.

Sector 17. His rescue mission.

"The intel is correct. Heat sensors indicate seven bodies."

It was Bryn. He and Von were dressed in full uniform with their ion blasters out of the thigh holsters, gripped tight in their hands. Black helmets were on their heads with strange visors. I felt the tension between them and the three other soldiers.

"Good. You've all seen the layout of this level. No Hive

has been here in three hours. We don't have a lot of time. Complete your task and report back to this location for transport out."

Everyone nodded at Von's command. He glanced at Bryn, saw his focused expression. They were about to go into danger. I sensed it, knew it, and wanted to reach out and stop him. But there was nothing I could do. This wasn't like the previous dreams where Von interacted with me. He wasn't *with* me this time. He was opening his mind, letting me see into his head, his thoughts. What made him Von.

"Let's get this done so Von here can go back to his mate," Bryn said. "Every second we're gone keeps him from claiming her."

Von grinned. "Damn right. Everyone ready?"

Another nod. "Let's do our jobs."

They raised their weapons and went into fight mode. Bryn and Von split off from the others, all with tasks to complete on this mission. Down a long corridor they went, waiting at turns to ensure there were no Hive.

God, the Hive could appear at any time and kill them! I'd heard they transported anywhere, in and out, capturing Coalition fighters and turning them into something like cyborgs—and that was if they survived.

I wanted to cry out to Von to go back, just to transport out, but he couldn't hear me.

Bryn stopped at a door, looked at some kind of display on his arm. "This is it."

Von nodded, then shot at the wall to the right of it. He waited a moment for the smoke to clear, then reached in, fiddled with some wires. Within a few seconds the door slid open silently.

Von entered first and through his eyes I could see women and children. Their intel had been correct. I counted seven.

Four women and three small children. They were huddled together in the corner, the little ones unnaturally subdued as the women used their bodies to shield them.

"Lady Nerum. Ladies." Von bowed slightly to them. "I am Senior Hunter Von. Commander Grigg sent us to retrieve you. Do not fear. You are safe now. We will see you safely back to your mates."

Bryn knelt down before them. "Is anyone hurt?"

The woman Von had addressed as Lady Nerum was clearly the leader of the group. She was nearly as tall as Von, her hair and skin an odd gold color I'd never seen with my own eyes. I'd seen pictures though, back at the Brides Processing Center. Prillon Prime had golden-skinned people with the sharp features and oddly slanted eyes. She was lovely, and strong as she stood and gathered the other women close.

"Hunters," she said the word like Von and his men were walking miracles. Another woman muffled a joy-filled cry with her hand, her relief palpable. All the women stood as Bryn aided them, Lady Nerum gripping a small boy tightly to her side.

Bryn held out his hand to the woman nearest him. "Come. We are taking you home."

The children were big enough to walk on their own but held the women's hands or the long length of their dresses.

Shots rang out from far away, the women cringed, clung to their children as Von led them through dark gray corridors. A shout sounded in Von's headpiece, loud enough for all the women to hear as Von whipped his head about. "We must go. Now."

He led the group, Bryn taking the rear.

Three Hive Scouts came around the corner directly ahead of Von, their strange silver skin and metallic eyes making them look like walking metal, despite the fact the closest Hive's face was shaped like a human. The other two were clearly of different races, one Prillon, his non-silver skin a striking orange tone. The third was an odd blue, and I took the knowledge from Von's mind that he was once a warrior from a planet called Xerima, a cold planet of extremes, of ice and volcanic activity.

Von was shocked to see him, as Xerima was under Coalition protection, but did not yet send warriors or brides to the war. Their people were considered too barbaric and uncivilized. The Atlans in particular, their closest planetary neighbor, did not get along well with the blue-skinned race.

Whatever the hell an Atlan was. All I could remember was Von shouted a warning to Bryn, was that the Atlans turned into some kind of beast. Which sounded scary.

Von fired his weapon, but the closest Hive, the one who looked like an average brown-haired human back home, kept walking like the hit did nothing.

The closer he got, the more I noticed the shimmering silver slivers that seemed to be alive and moving under his skin like tiny worms. They covered his neck and half his head. One eye was completely silver, like mercury in a meat thermometer, and he never blinked, just kept walking.

"Fuck. Get them out of here, Bryn!" Von shouted the command and took a couple steps back, but bumped into Lady Nerum.

"I've got three!" Bryn shouted back and fired his own weapon.

"Ladies, get down!" Von bellowed as he rose and charged the Hive, firing repeatedly into the creature's head until he toppled over, his skull actually sizzling as Von stepped over his twitching body. "Stay down!"

He risked a glance over his shoulder and met Lady

Nerum's gaze. She nodded as Hive shots raced over her head in both directions. Bryn bellowed from behind them as Von yelled curses into his comms. "We've got the package. Pinned down in corridor three."

"We're coming." The voice was barely heard over the sound of the Hive's heavy booted footsteps. With their first man down, the remaining two Hive focused on Von with an intensity that made me shiver.

"We will kill you now." The blue one spoke and his voice was menacing.

Von actually chuckled, which made me want to scream at him to run, to get out of there.

Instead, he pulled two long knives from inside his boots and stood slowly. "Come and get me, boys."

The Hive charged, but Von moved too fast to track. He vanished like a ghost in a streak of darkness. The black armor he wore made him nothing more than a hint of a shadow.

Holy shit. My man could *move.*

Earth media downplayed the Hive, made them out to be like some kind of TV sci-fi bad guy. Scary the way dragons or wizards were scary, as in not really *real.* While we were told that they were dangerous, they'd been light years away from Earth.

This Hive? He wasn't far away at all. Only a few feet in front of Von with his own weapon out and firing on my mate.

I screamed, but no one heard me.

The two Hive dropped, blood splattering from the backs of their necks. Behind them, my mate reappeared, his knives wet from using them to sever their spinal columns with his blades.

"Bryn?" he shouted.

"Clear. Let's go."

Von hurried to the ladies and helped them to their feet, Bryn assisting. "Carry the children. We need to run. These Scouts are dead, but the Hive will transport replacements. We need to hurry." Lifting his hand to his helmet, he addressed his other team members.

"You're too slow. We're clear. Meet at extraction point."

"Confirmed. Meet at extraction point for transport."

His long legs ate up the distance to the meeting point as the women hurried along behind them. I wondered why Von didn't carry one of the children, but realized if they met more Hive, he'd have his hands full of babies and not be able to fight.

"We clear for transport?" he called to the other three Hunters who waited. One was bloody and the others were coated in black as if they'd come in contact with some kind of fire.

One of them nodded. "Cleared and ready."

"Transport for twelve. Now."

Shots were fired as I felt the swirling blue pull of the transport. I heard a shout, a cry of a child, Von's yelling as fire burned through his shoulder.

He'd been hit!

"No!" I cried, shooting upright in bed, the sheet wrapped around me. I was breathing hard, my body laced with sweat. It had been a dream. Only a dream. Why hadn't Von come to me in my dream and made love to me instead of...that?

As I caught my breath, looking at the plain walls of my room, noting the soft carpeting on the floor, the doorway to the bathroom, my window with the curtains closed on the opposite wall. I ensured I was safe, that I wasn't in some stark corridor on a Hive controlled ship.

Was Von even awake? Had he intentionally showed me

his mission? Did he want me to see that? Or had his mental walls crumbled, exposing his mind to me in ways he had not anticipated? Would he even know I'd shared his nightmare? Talking to him, mind to mind while we dreamed was one thing. But entering his mind? Experiencing what he saw and felt and knew? That was something different.

If I dreamt of tending to my dying father, would Von be there? Smelling the scent of death on my father's skin? See the blank, glassy gaze of a man who no longer recognized his own daughter, no longer remembered his own name? Would Von feel my pain? Experience my grief? Was this new link between us created because we were almost fully mated now? With each passing day, the need between us grew, the bond became more intense.

Pushing the sheets aside, I rose and walked to the window, the flowing beauty of my nightgown a stark contrast to the horror I'd just witnessed. I pulled back the curtains and stared up at the two moons of Everis. They hung in the sky like two shining balls on a Christmas tree, one partially obscured by the other. Incar was smaller, a pale silvery white, not unlike our own moon. I'd read that Incar was used as a prison colony and held the most dangerous criminals in the entire universe. The Coalition Fleet had built their prison here because it was the renowned Hunters who usually brought them to justice.

The second moon, Seladon, hung like a pale green orb, not dark like fresh grass, but like those little green mints served at a wedding. Pastel green. That moon had been colonized hundreds of years ago by people from Everis and was an active and vibrant farming colony. They supplied much of the planet with fresh food and took the rest to undeveloped worlds, worlds like Xerima…and Earth. Worlds too *primitive* and *volatile* to have achieved full admission into the Interstellar Coalition.

The light of the two moons blotted out almost all the stars I could normally see on a clear night, not that it mattered. I did not recognize any of the constellations. The moons hung, large and strange over the horizon taunting me with their strangeness as the memory of those Hive soldiers made me shiver.

For the first time since I'd begun this crazy adventure, I truly felt like I was on an alien world.

Von wasn't just wandering about the countryside like a sheriff's deputy keeping everyone safe. He wasn't a mall security guard. He was a Senior Hunter of an advanced race, a respected member of the Coalition Fleet. He was both honorable and feared. He saved people from harm. From danger. From a fate worse than death.

He was like some kind of superhero, fast, brave and strong and...*mine.*

Fixing the sheets, I settled back in bed and willed myself to sleep. I wanted to go to him in my dreams, knowing that was the only way I could be with him in this moment.

He couldn't come into our suite and while I could go to his, I remembered his words. I didn't want him to claim me until there was no doubt in his mind as to my reason. When I made him mine forever, it wouldn't be because I was worried about Major Cosmo. It would be because I wanted him to be mine. Forever.

———

Lexi

. . .

"I CAN'T BELIEVE HE DOESN'T WANT YOU THERE," DANI SAID. She was putting her long hair up into a ponytail, then twirling it into a bun. It seemed to be her morning routine. While her blonde hair was pretty down, she seemed to prefer it up.

I shrugged, plopping down on the couch in my Everian pajamas—a long-sleeved, flowing pearl-colored nightgown that made me feel like a princess. I never wore stuff like this back home, usually sleeping in a pair of pajama shorts and a cami in summer, and leggings and a T-shirt in winter. The suite had one main room with a small kitchen, then three bedrooms with private bathrooms.

She and Katie had been asleep when I came in the night before so this was the first they'd heard of the challenge and his wanting me to remain here, in our suite, when he fought Cosmo.

I was late to get up, the dream Von had shared, most likely unintentionally, had me tossing and turning. He was very determined to keep me from seeing the underbelly of life out here, in space. The Hive, even Major Cosmo. While there was no similarity between the evilness of the two—the major was just a pest and nothing more—Von considered all threats to me unacceptable. I felt that conviction within him in the dream, the protective streak that was more than societal or logical. His need to shelter me from everything, even a frightening dream, was instinctive, hardwired into his genetic makeup and he took the whole thing to an extreme level of seriousness.

But I understood him a bit better now. He had seen horrible things, used his gifts to fight and keep people safe. But that was people, in the abstract. I was *his*. I felt the difference every time he looked at me, in the way he touched me. He gave me a sense of safety I'd ever known in my entire life, and I was tempted to surrender to that comfort and just give him control. But then my stubborn *padre*'s voice would rise up. I came from a proud people, a people who were explorers and conquerors. That was part of my DNA too, and that independent streak wasn't going to go away, especially when something was important to me. Like Von... and this stupid challenge.

With the sun up and definite bags under my eyes, I sat and thought about him some more. I didn't need to be sheltered from life. Yes, I was inexperienced, a virgin, but I wasn't an idiot. I'd survived losing my parents and had the courage to transport across the universe to become an Interstellar Bride, give myself to an alien I'd never even met.

I wasn't a coward or a child to be sheltered. I wanted to know that the major would no longer be a threat. I wanted to see it with my own eyes. And I really wanted to be there if Von needed me. If I was truly his mate, then I could offer him support in ways no one else could.

With the girls already up and eager to hear about my night, I shared.

Not everything. But we talked about the dance and our dresses. Dani had fended off more than one interested suitor, determined to give her mate time to come to her. Katie looked like she'd had an adventurous night, but she was surprisingly tight-lipped about Bryn and what was going on between them.

I told them about the marks on my arm and how Von had noticed them, how he'd taken the scent of Cosmo off my arm like a bloodhound and seemed to know exactly where Cosmo was standing in the ballroom.

They were both extremely interested in that little bit of information. We had no idea what these men of ours were capable of, not really. We knew they were Hunters, respected and feared across the entire Coalition Fleet, but we didn't understand *why*.

And then I told them about the dream, about the way Von had moved so quickly I'd lost track of him. How he'd reappeared *behind* the Hive soldiers, their spinal columns severed before they even knew he'd moved.

"So, maybe they're like werewolves, but they just don't change their shape." Dani sat on the chair opposite me, her dainty legs tucked up under her body as she sipped her tea. Her nightgown was a navy that made her look like a dark angel with her halo of golden hair.

Katie laughed at her. "You are such a weirdo."

Dani shrugged, but her grin was downright impish. "Come on. Admit it. You were totally on team Jacob like every reasonable woman on the planet." She sipped her tea and leaned her head back with a very feminine groan of appreciation, her eyes closed. "Werewolves are totally hot. Or Michael, in *Underworld*. Do me, baby."

"They're not werewolves." I giggled a bit, remembering the way Von had lowered his face to my skin and taken my scent into his lungs.

"No, they're just aliens." Katie lifted her feet to rest them on the small table in the center, her ankles crossed. "Horny aliens."

That got Dani's attention. "Do tell, Katie. You're like Fort Knox over there. I saw you with Bryn last night. How's it going?"

Katie shrugged. "I'm so not going there. Lexi?"

I shook my head. No freaking way. I was *not* giving them details. I could barely believe the way I'd acted last night, the feel of Von's cock filling my ass, stretching me open. I'd come all over him, more than once, barely able to breathe and begging for more. He made me crazy, like lose-my-freaking-mind and all self-control crazy. Nope. Not going there.

I shifted on the couch, my bottom still a little tender. No, my private time with Von wasn't something I was going to recount. I did tell them about Major Cosmo and the challenge that was scheduled for today. For once, I was glad for it because it completely distracted Katie and Dani from further inquiries into my sex life and me from that terrifying dream.

"Why shouldn't you go to the fight?" Katie asked, taking a sip of something close to coffee. She sat on the opposite end of the couch wearing a similar nightgown, but hers was a pale blue that matched her eyes. "He's going to win. The major is a weakling in comparison to Von."

"He said he couldn't protect me if I was there and he was busy fighting."

Katie shrugged. "That seems a little...possessive."

I snorted at that. Possessive? That word times ten.

"Protect you? From what?" Katie asked. "We'll be just outside the Touchstone and we'll be with you. There are guards everywhere. It's not like you'd be going off alone to a strange planet."

True, we'd yet to leave the building. We knew nothing of Everis other than what I could see from my window or read about in their books. I hoped once Von claimed me, I'd see it. I wanted to see everything here. I wondered what the animals were like, and the trees? What did their flowers smell like? Was their grass green? Did they have orchards and farms on the planet or was it all grown on their moon? Did chefs here plant their own gardens? Did they even have chefs? Maybe they grew their food indoors, under grow lights like hydroponic farms back on Earth.

"And she's not going to go to the challenge to pick up another guy," Dani added. "It's not like she's trolling."

I wasn't. I didn't want anyone else. I only wanted Von. I only wanted what he'd said he'd do to me after the challenge. Claim me, make me his completely. My nipples tightened and my pussy clenched in anticipation. I remembered how thick and big he was when he'd carefully slipped into my ass. I couldn't wait to find out how fantastic he'd feel stretching me open and taking my virginity.

"She's going to see her man get all hot and sweaty, fighting another alien for her. It's chest thumping and basic Neanderthal behavior. I, for one, don't miss out on that kind of testosterone-fest," Dani added.

Dani did have a point. The idea of Von fighting someone else for me—*me!*—was actually pretty hot. Like ruined-panties hot.

"Fine, Von going all caveman makes her ovaries jump for joy," Katie said, getting up to go refill her mug. "But he's a bossy alien and shouldn't tell her what she can or can't do. That's the main reason we should go. Let him boss you now and he'll think he can boss you forever. You have to set the tone for the whole relationship now."

I glanced at Dani, who looked elegant and perfect, even sprawled out on the couch next to me. She shrugged her dainty shoulders as she glanced my way. "She does have a point. I mean, if you're to be with him forever and all that, you need to show him exactly who is going to be in charge of Alexis Lopez."

"Me," I said.

"You," Katie added, settling back down and blowing on her hot drink before taking a sip. "My mother always said, start a relationship how you want it to go otherwise you'll be picking dirty socks off the floor and falling into the toilet because the seat's left up for the rest of your life."

Von and I hadn't gotten to the dirty socks part of our relationship. No, only hot oral action in a restaurant and anal sex on the second date. I got their point though. If I let Von walk all over me now, he'd do it for the rest of our lives. Sure, I'd let him protect me from real threats, but just watching him beat up Major Cosmo? I didn't see the danger.

"You'll both go with me, right? It's not like I would go alone," I said, glancing between them. They both nodded.

"We wouldn't miss it. That major? He's a creep. I'd love to see him get punched in the nose," Dani added. For someone so small, she was pretty ruthless.

I stood up and both girls looked to me. "We're going."

Katie and Dani also stood, grinning.

"We're going," Katie repeated.

"Hell, yeah."

exi

I THOUGHT THE FIGHT WOULD BE LIKE A BOXING MATCH, IN A ring with a referee. Gloves. Maybe even something like the ridiculous wrestling shows on TV but without the men in tights. This? This was insane.

It wasn't within the walls of the Touchstone, but in an open courtyard below the hilltop. The three of us had followed the numbers of males who were headed to the fight. At first, we hadn't known where to go, but we eavesdropped on multiple conversations so it wasn't too tough to figure out that we were headed in the right direction.

Everian males lined the outer edges of the large space, probably half the size of a football field. Most of the men wore uniforms I was by now very familiar with in brown and navy. Those who weren't in the military wore various colored pants and white shirts. Simple clothes but they did not hide the fact that Everian males were big. So much bigger than most Earth men. Like football linebacker big. And tall.

While we were waiting for Von and Major Cosmo to show up, the gathered men stared at us. Blatantly and openly, like we were the aliens and they couldn't quite figure out what we were doing there.

We made our way up to the perimeter, marked by odd sticks placed in the ground about every ten or fifteen paces. I reached out to touch one of them but my hand met solid resistance, and I realized there was a force field around the area, but I wasn't sure if it was designed to keep the combatants in or the rest of the yelling men out.

Katie lifted her hand to test the force field for herself before leaning in to me to whisper, "Have you noticed we are the only women here?"

Um, yeah. Where were the other matched women? If this kind of a brawl was going on back home, there would be women everywhere, right next to the men.

The male on our right was a large man in a brown uniform. He reached out and touched Dani on the shoulder, not roughly, just to get her attention. She jumped back and bumped into Katie, then me. We didn't fall, but Katie stepped on my foot and she was wearing boots, with heels. Damn it.

"Ow!" I shoved her away from me.

"Sorry," Kate mumbled, regaining her footing. We both scowled at the man who'd started the whole thing. Dani had her hands on her hips and glared up at him like a toy poodle staring down a Rottweiler.

"Watch it, buster," Dani said.

"My name is not Buster, but you can call me anything you'd like," the man said, clearly interested in Dani.

"I don't think so," she countered.

Before the conversation could get any worse, cheering broke out in the crowd. We looked up and even Buster forgot about Dani, at least for the moment, to watch as Von entered the courtyard from our left, Major Cosmo from the right, like gladiators walking toward each other from opposite ends of the arena. They wore nothing but their pants. No weapon holster on their thighs. Von's pants were brown, Cosmo's blue, and both men's chests were bare.

"Oh my God, they're huge." Dani sounded stunned, but I'd had my hands on my mate, danced with him, felt his massive chest and arms, his thick thighs.

"Yes, they are," Katie confirmed and looked at me, wiggling her eyebrows. I grinned back. I was pretty sure Katie wasn't talking about their shoulders.

The look on Von's face was of a hardened warrior. I remembered the dream, the dangerous mission, the terror. He'd focused his mind on the task, blocked out everything else and went to work with a similar expression. Was he doing this now? Blocking out everything and getting his mission done? To take down Major Cosmo.

He'd touched me, bruised my arm, expressed his interest in making me his mate. It went deeper than that though. This was a lifelong grudge that would come to a head now. Because of me.

Von wouldn't kill the major, but I knew he wanted to make sure Cosmo never touched me again. He wanted every other man on the planet to know I belonged to him, was under his protection. Von was a very possessive mate.

He was here, fighting because of me. For me.

One second they were twenty feet apart, fists clenched, and in the blink of an eye they were on each other.

"Whoa," Katie said. "Did you see that? How did they—"

"How can they move so fast?" Dani asked, her voice laced with awe.

Buster spoke up. "Earth aliens don't move that quickly?" When Dani gave him a look that screamed, *Duh* he continued. "Hunters can move faster than your eyes can track. Most of us have learned to rein it in, to use our speed and strength only when riled. Like now. Those two are using all that energy, that speed, to win."

I didn't like what he'd said. It was as if my eyes had hit the fast-forward button and the men moved with an unnatural speed. I heard fists connect with bone, but couldn't see it, my eyes and brain not processing quickly enough.

They came apart, circled. Breathing hard, their chests rose and fell. The major's face was coated in sweat and there was a cut above his right eye. Von had bloody knuckles on his left hand.

They were going to beat the shit out of each other no matter how fast they moved. I just couldn't see it happen.

"He's fighting for your honor, and yet you chose to be here. I wonder if perhaps he has made a mistake?" a deep voice beside me asked. A very large hand neared my head, his fingers trailing through a strand of my long black hair where it blew around my face in the slight breeze. "Or if you really are special?"

I glanced up and I saw an Everian eyeing me with a very male, very interested grin on his face. His hand stroked down my arm and I stepped back. Von had caressed me like that and I'd loved his touch, but this felt like a complete violation of my personal space.

He didn't let me get far, his hand closed on my wrist.

"Let me go," I said, my voice slow and clear.

He did, but my relief was short lived. His grip slid to my

fingers and he bent low, kissing the back of my hand and my wrist with a little too much lingering, and tasting.

Ew! Gross? Had he just licked me?

"Stop that!" I said, yanking on my hand, trying to get away.

A collective gasp came from the crowd and I looked up. Von had stilled and turned toward me. He'd heard me over the noise of the crowd, over everything. His eyes widened, then flared with anger at the sight of this guy touching me.

Cosmo took advantage of the distraction to punch him. He drew his arm back slowly, so slowly that I saw the strike coming and tried to scream a warning. "Look out!"

Von ignored Cosmo completely, his complete focus on me and the man touching me still. The major's punch landed with a loud crack and both men went flying, Von from the punch, and Cosmo from the force of the strike behind it. I heard the crack, saw Von's head rock to the side. Even then, his eyes remained trained on me.

"Von!" I screamed.

His gaze held mine a second longer, even after being stunned by the blow. A growl ripped from his chest and he turned to the major. His pace sped up, and he flew through the air. Sounds of fighting came to me but all I saw was a blur. It lasted forever, it seemed to me, but was probably only a second or two. Major Cosmo was on the ground, unconscious. Von loomed over him, arms raised to the sky as he yelled into the air like a crazed man.

The moment his roar of challenge, of victory, ended, he turned and moved to me in a blink of an eye. He lifted one of the markers that maintained the barrier and tossed it behind him like a stick.

"You are touching my mate," Von murmured, his voice low and deadly.

The Everian male's hand slipped from me. I was impressed he hadn't run away or peed himself. Von was barely breathing hard, his rock-hard chest glistening under the bright light of their sun. He looked good enough to jump on the spot, so sexy I felt hot all over just admiring all that fabulous muscle and power. Mine. He was mine. But he was far from pleased. The look in his eyes alone should have killed the man.

"She was unaccompanied at a challenge," the man replied.

"Do you wish to challenge me for her? If you do, I will tell you now that you'll look worse than him." Von angled his head toward the unmoving major. "Challenge me and I'll break you."

"You should keep her under control, Hunter," the idiot repeated. Why didn't he just give up?

"Major Cosmo put his hand on her arm. You had your mouth on her flesh. Do you really wish to die today? She is my marked mate."

The guy's eyes widened and I swear he went white as a sheet. "You share marks?"

"Yes."

The man's attitude changed completely in the blink of an eye and he bowed his head to Von and stepped back. "My apologies." After bowing to me, he turned and walked away without a backward glance.

"She wasn't unaccompanied. I was with her," Katie said.

"Me, too," Dani added.

"Yet none of you are accompanied by a guard or protector," Von countered.

A guard? We needed a freaking man to chaperone us? I glanced away, took in the Everians all staring at the three of us girls.

Well, okay. Yeah, maybe we were like little baby bunnies

surrounded by a courtyard full of wolves. Maybe this hadn't been a good idea after all.

"I will attend to Katie and her friend."

The voice came from behind me and Von glanced over my shoulder. "Bryn, good. See that they are safely escorted back to the Cornerstone."

Von took a step closer, ignoring everyone and everything around us. "You, mate, are coming with me." While his gaze hadn't lost any of the hardness or anger, his hold on my wrist was remarkably gentle and the heat of his touch sent a sizzle of lust through my body.

I quickened my pace to follow him as he pulled me along beside him, the onlookers parting to let us by. As we went, I glanced back at Cosmo, who was slowly coming to, a few of the warriors hovering over him and tending to his wounds. He wasn't a threat anymore. Von had defeated him easily and I wondered why he'd denied the challenge for so long. "He really never was a threat to you, was he?"

Von glanced back over his shoulder and I saw something close to pity in his gaze. "No. I explained this fact to you last night."

"Did he know that?"

"Of course."

"Then why did he challenge you?"

"Pride is a dangerous thing, Lexi. A woman wounded both his pride and his heart when she chose me. We were barely more than boys, but he loved her and she betrayed him. A warrior cannot hate the woman he loves, and so—"

"He hated you instead." My anger at Cosmo softened into something closer to empathy, sorrow, perhaps even pity.

"Yes. There are things a man can live with, and things he cannot."

"So now what happens between you?"

"Now he has finally made his strike at me. His honor has been appeased. His rage will fade. Now he will rest. It is over." He pulled me closer and wrapped his arm around me. "Now, I make you mine."

Yeah, they were Neanderthals, but I was, in this moment, content to be a cavewoman. Von was dragging me off to his cave, fortunately not by the hair.

———

Von

IT WAS VERY DIFFICULT TO REMAIN CALM WITH LEXI AFTER THE fight. My focus and anger had been solely on Cosmo, ending our long-term feud once and for all. But then I'd heard her. My Lexi. Just one word and I knew she was in trouble. Cosmo was a fighter, not as good as me, but still skilled and powerful. I shouldn't have looked away, but nothing would deter me from my mate. Not when she was in trouble. I knew something was wrong when I heard the tone of her voice. Cosmo had taken advantage of my distraction and landed a solid punch. I'd seen spots from it, but there was no way I would be taken down when Lexi needed me.

And that Hunter's hand on her body? His lips caressing her skin? The asshole was lucky to still have his face attached to his skull.

My need to claim her...finally claim her, was greater than the need to track him down and beat him into a pulp. That fool would sleep alone tonight.

But Lexi was mine.

Sliding my hand down, I tangled our fingers together as I led her to my room. I slowed when I realized she was practically running, but did not stop until we were behind the closed and locked door.

My cock was hard, a result of the fight, but also knowing the last impediment in the way of making Lexi mine was gone.

She stood before me, her breathing ragged, her eyes wide and a tad tentative, but not fearful. The dress she wore was short, falling to her knees, the color a soft pink. It was a perfect match color of the blush on her cheeks, of her innocence. The dress covered her breasts and had short sleeves, but I could see every curve. I remembered every decadent inch of her. She licked her lips when she saw the outline of my cock where it pressed against my uniform pants.

"Do you want to be mine? Forever, Lexi. This is forever."

Her eyes met mine and she nodded, but that wasn't enough. Not this time.

"Say it." I wanted to hear the words, to know she wanted to be mine. After this there would be no going back. I wanted to be absolutely certain she wanted me as much as I wanted her. Forever.

"I…I want you to be mine forever."

"There's no going back, Lexi." I needed to say it, give her one final chance to back out, because once I touched her, I wouldn't want to stop.

"I don't want to go back. I want to be yours."

"I may not have claimed all of you—yet—but you're already mine." I took a step toward her. Heat flared in her eyes and I watched as her nipples tightened.

"Yes."

"Then the only thing standing between us now is your punishment."

She frowned and took a step back, bumped into the door. "Punishment?"

I growled, thinking of that Hunter's hand on her, of her walking to the challenge field unprotected.

"Punishment," I repeated, stalking toward her. "For your deliberate disobedience and disregard for your safety."

"I'm sorry. I didn't know. I didn't understand."

"I know, mate." I walked to her and cupped her cheek in my hand, my body still vibrating with the need to fight, or fuck. Maybe both. I itched to get her over my lap, to see her pale ass quiver beneath the strike of my palm, to see my handprint bloom a bright pink on her soft skin. "But you should have listened to me. You are on a strange world. You do not know our culture or customs. I told you to remain in your suite because I needed to know you were safe."

She leaned into my touch, which soothed my wildness, helped calm my racing heart. She was here. She was safe. And she was mine forever.

"I wanted to see you fight, to know that you weren't hurt. I was so afraid you were hurt. I just…I needed to see you."

Her gaze darted away and I knew there was something she hid from me. "Lexi?"

"I… I saw you in a dream. I saw everything that happened. How you rescued those women and children. I saw the Hive creatures and how you…disappeared and sliced open their spines. I saw how brave you are and I felt you get shot when you transported. My shoulder was on fire." Her gaze drifted to my chest and shoulder, clearly looking for an injury that was no longer there. That blaster wound had been healed quickly with a ReGen wand after we returned from the mission.

She'd been sharing my mind as I fought the Hive on that ship? She felt my pain when their weapons struck me?

By the Divine, I wanted to protect her, not drag her into battle with me. "No." I leaned forward until our foreheads touched. "I don't want that for you."

She lifted her gaze and the tenderness I saw there, the love, made my knees weak. I'd expected to win her heart by conquering her body, by giving her so much pleasure that she'd never want the touch of another.

I had not expected her to see everything. In that moment I became truly vulnerable, standing before her, awaiting judgment.

I hunted. I killed. That side of me was part of my nature, part of my reason for being. Yes, I served the Coalition Fleet and my people, did things no one else could do. But that did not mean the reality of my life would be any easier for her to bear. I had foolishly assumed I could keep her from knowing the darkness in me. She was goodness and life, innocence and warmth. If she turned from me now, I wasn't sure I could survive the loss.

"Lexi." Her name. It was the only word I had, and a lifetime of longing, of loneliness, went into it.

"It's true. I wanted to see the challenge, to see you beat the major." She lifted her hands to my face, holding my jaw, keeping me close, so close our breaths mingled in the small space between us. "But in reality, I couldn't bear to wait until later to see you. I felt you get hurt and I...I needed to know you were okay. I'm yours, Von. But you're mine, too."

Lexi went up on her tiptoes and kissed me, the first time she'd initiated our contact, the first time she'd made love to me. With a soft moan, I wrapped my arms around her and crushed her to me as she molded her body to mine.

Yes. This was what I needed. My mate, warm and responsive in my arms, offering me solace and acceptance, offering me everything.

Forcing myself to end the kiss, I took her wrist and led her to the bed, felt the thrum of her rapid pulse.

"That wasn't a dream, but a nightmare. Somehow you were with me on our mission. I didn't want that for you, but it seems marked mates can't keep much of anything from each other."

I sat on the edge of my bed and pulled her to stand between my parted knees. She was at just the right height for me to take a hard nipple into my mouth.

"After the dr...nightmare, I have complete faith in your abilities. I'm sorry I didn't understand about today. I didn't mean to place myself in danger, but you can't hide me away to keep me safe."

"Yes, I can," I countered, moving my hands to her narrow waist.

"No, Von. Maybe you don't understand what it means to have a mate. I will worry about you. I will be afraid for you, no matter how skilled you are in battle. And I was with my friends. I assumed the only person who might be in danger at the challenge was you."

"You doubt my abilities," I grumbled.

"No. I'm in love with you. You're mine. You worry about me, I worry about you. That's how it works."

"Yes, but your worries were unfounded," I added, thinking of how weak Cosmo was. "Cosmo was no threat to me."

"I understand that now. But I wanted to see you and make sure you were all right. I didn't know the others would get all handsy."

"You are an unclaimed female. You are beautiful. You were alone." I covered her lips with my fingers when she opened her mouth to protest. "Before you say Katie and Dani were with you, they, too, are unclaimed and unprotected.

The company of another unmated female does not shield you from the advances or seductions of eager potential mates."

"Yes, I understand now."

"So you will be spanked for not listening to me."

She tried to step back but I held fast.

"I will not," she said, her voice very adamant.

I slid my hands down her legs over her dress until I reached the hem, then changed directions and worked my way back up, this time on her bare skin. Higher and higher I went until I cupped her bottom. Her bare bottom.

"You went to a challenge with your pussy bare?" I barked.

This pussy was *mine*.

"I... I did it for you, so after—"

Her words cooled my anger, but made my balls ache.

Pushing the dress up, I lifted it over her head, dropped it to the floor with all the haste of an eager lover.

My breath hissed out as I looked my fill. Pale skin, upturned breasts, tight nipples, slightly rounded belly, flared hips, perfect pussy.

"After, what? What did you hope would occur?"

"I hoped you would claim me, make me yours." Her voice got quiet, perhaps even shy. She had not yet learned to tell me exactly what she needed, but she would, in time. Someday I hoped to return home to find her sprawled naked in my bed with her legs open wide. She would smile and lift her breasts, and beg me to make her scream.

"You're so beautiful, mate. Perfect," I murmured as I nuzzled her breast. Her fingers rose to tangle in my hair and hold me to her. The gesture soothed me as nothing else could. The scent of her welcoming heat drifted to me, the sweetness of her skin a balm to my senses. But it was her touch, filled with such love and trust, that unmade me. I would do anything for this woman. Fight. Kill. Beg. Steal. Break my vows to the other Hunters and the Fleet. I would lie down and die in her place with no question, and the intensity of the feeling running through me made me tremble.

"So you're not going to spank me?"

I lifted my hand and brought it down on the fleshy part of her ass.

She startled and gripped my shoulders.

"I am," I replied. The swat hadn't been hard, more to get her attention focused on what she'd done. Mine, too. Just looking at her body, knowing her taste, had me redirecting my thoughts.

"But—"

I spanked her other ass cheek.

"Von!"

I soothed the heated flesh, then slid my fingers down between her thighs.

"Soaked. Just as I thought."

Her hips curled toward me, probably against her mind's wishes. Her body knew what it wanted and it wanted to be dominated, adored, it wanted to feel a small bite of pain with its pleasure.

"You like the sting. It makes you wet."

She shook her head.

Spank.

"You do. Your pussy's dripping."

Spank. Spank.

"Von," she said again, this time with breathless anticipation.

"You don't want a weak mate. You like knowing I will watch out for you, protect you. Keep you in line. I will always take care of you, whether it's to lick your pussy or spank your ass for stirring up trouble."

That earned me a bit of laughter, the sound full of happiness and breathless anticipation. "If you're done playing with my ass, I'd rather you lick my pussy."

A groan escaped and I narrowed my eyes at her. "You are a very naughty girl."

Spank.

Spank.

Lifting her up, I turned and tossed her onto the bed. She bounced once before coming up onto her elbows, legs parted slightly. She stared up at me completely unaware of her allure. Stunning. Hair wild about her head, her cheeks flushed, her eyes passionate and full of challenge.

I hadn't even claimed her yet. How full of fire and passion would she be once she knew her own limits, when she was comfortable with our bodies, with giving and receiving pleasure.

I opened my pants then and my cock sprang free. A sigh escaped, the pressure gone, but not the need. "I'm weak around you. My cock, it's always hard."

I gripped the base and stroked up and down, easing some of the tension coiling in me. My thumb slipped over the drop of fluid that slid from the tip.

"Look at me, Lexi. Look at me and tell me who has all the power."

Slyly, she glanced down at my cock, at my straining muscles, the tremors rocking my body with desire.

"I think I do," she replied.

"You're right, mate." I squeezed my cock. "This? It's for you. Only for you. Me? I'm all yours. Only yours. Forever."

Lexi came up onto her knees before me on the raised bed and our bodies aligned, chest to chest, thigh to thigh. I loosened my hold, then let go completely when she put her hand over mine and took over stroking me. It was hard to keep my knees from buckling at the feel of her small grip.

"Harder."

Her eyes drifted down my body.

"I'm weak for you. Powerless."

"Von," she whispered.

"Will you take me as your marked mate, let me claim you, body and mind?" I could hear the tinge of vulnerability in my voice. A simple "no" from her would finish me. I'd be nothing.

Perhaps she saw my weakness. With her free hand, she touched my mark on the side of my chest. So very softly. "Heart, too."

Heart? Yes.

I felt the mark heat and she gasped. Yes, *she* gasped when she touched me.

"Feel that, do you?" I asked, touching her in the identical place, on the identical mark she bore. "This mark made you mine from birth. I've always been yours. Always."

Lexi looked at me, released her hold, lowered herself to the bed so her head was on the pillows. As I watched, she parted her legs, bent her knees. One hand went to her breast and cupped it like an offering. It was my fantasy come to life.

"I'm yours. Claim me. Claim my pussy. Fill me with your seed."

17

OH. MY. GOD.

I had the hottest guy in the universe looming over me, his hand gripping and stroking his large cock as he looked me over. And I mean *looked me over* like a wolf ready to eat his prey.

And I hoped he did. I even parted my thighs a little more so he got the hint.

This was it. I was going to give my virginity to Von.

I had no doubts, no worries, not even a blip in my mind about whether or not this was the right thing to do.

Guys on Earth had been a waste of my time. I could see that clearly now. I hadn't been interested in any of them because I hadn't felt like this. It hadn't been Von.

They'd all wanted a body to fuck. Just a way to get off. Sex with any of them would have meant nothing to them but a meaningless release. I'd have been fucked and left. None of them had wanted *me*.

Von wanted me. He wanted my body, too, but I knew it was so much more. My mark burned with intensity as if it somehow knew that this was it. The moment when we'd finally be one.

Putting one knee on the bed, Von crawled over me, holding himself up with a forearm he placed near my head. He stroked my hair back from my face, then slid his fingers over the shell of my ear, down my neck, over my breast, my belly, waist, hip and then to my pussy.

All the while, his dark gaze held mine. He was touching my body, but his eyes were looking at me, seeing my reaction to his soft touch.

"You're soaked. Is that all for me? For my cock?" he murmured.

I nodded, licked my lips. Shifting my leg, I made room for him to settle his hips between mine.

"You still have your pants on," I whispered when I felt the coarse material of his uniform instead of his heated skin.

He grinned. "You're right. You make me forget everything...but this."

His hips rocked into me and the head of his cock slid over my slick, swollen flesh.

Pushing off, he stood at the foot of the bed and stripped out of his pants and boots and all the while I watched, my every sense tuned to the way he moved, the way he smelled, the way his muscles rippled just beneath his skin.

It was like my own private porno.

"Like what you see?" he asked, with his brow raised and the corner of his mouth tipped up.

I didn't respond, only crooked my finger.

"Where was I?" he asked, settling back into place. All he

had to do was shift his hips to put himself inside me. I felt the springy hair on his legs where they rubbed against mine. I was so aware of him that I breathed when he did, so focused on him that my body tuned itself to his. If I closed my eyes and focused on the mark, I would swear I could feel his heart beating there. I felt…everything.

"Not close enough," I replied, shifting my hips so the head of his cock parted my lower lips and settled at my virgin entrance. "I want you inside me."

"You're not ready for my cock, mate," he replied.

I frowned up at him. "I'm ready."

He shook his head and kissed me, making me forget why I thought I wasn't ready. I had no idea how long we kissed, but when he broke away and ran the rasp of his whiskers down my tender skin, all I could say was his name.

When his mouth sucked on my nipple, I couldn't even do that.

Fingers tangled in his hair, pulling him back at the intense feel of his mouth drawing on that turgid tip, then pushing him down farther, wanting more.

He switched sides, making me brainless with want.

I couldn't help but shift my hips, tilt them up to take him in.

He worked his way lower, ignoring me, ignoring everything but his focused attentions.

When his breath fanned over my slippery folds, his large hands settling on my thighs to keep them nice and wide for him, he said, "You'll come, mate. Then I'll fuck you. I'm big and your pussy will be very tight. I don't want to hurt you."

"Now, I'm ready now." His hot breath fanned over my heated core and I arched my hips off the bed, desperate for more.

"I'll tell you when you're ready."

I should have hated his bossiness, but his head was between my thighs. What woman would argue at a time like this? When he licked me from top to bottom and then latched on to my clit, I tangled my fingers in his hair once again and surrendered, holding on for the ride.

This time, he didn't just use his tongue, but slipped the tip of his finger into me.

"So tight," he murmured, then returned to pleasuring me with vigor.

I wanted him to go deeper, but it seemed he was just taunting me.

"More," I cried.

He lifted his head, slid his hand up to cup my breast and met my gaze. "No. I want you to be desperate for my cock to fill you up."

"Then do it," I snapped, flopping my head back on the bed.

I heard him chuckle just before his tongue flicked over me. "So needy. You want to come, mate?"

"Yes!"

"Then come. Now."

His words were followed by an all-out assault on my clit. Yes, he'd been taunting me before. Now, he took the tender flesh in his mouth and sucked, and at the same time, flicked his tongue over it.

"Oh my god," I moaned.

I was right there, floating on the very edge. When he moved his hand from my breast to cover my mark, heat flared, shooting like lightning from the mark to my core and I came.

I screamed.

I thrashed.

I begged.

I clenched down on the very tip of his finger.

I drowned in pleasure.

I was too far gone to realize he'd come up over me again.

"Now you're ready," he murmured, settling himself in place. "Look at me, Alexis Lopez from Earth. You are mine. I claim you as my marked mate."

"Yes," hissed out as he slowly filled me, stretching me open with one long, thick stroke. He didn't stop, wasn't tentative, but gained entry one inch at a time until he was buried balls deep, his cock bumping the tip of my womb.

Von's eyes were on me, watching me closely, as if he were memorizing this moment. I was too caught up in the feel of it, my body's adjustment to having him inside. I'd had his cock in my mouth and I knew it was big, but having him… there felt like *more.*

I wiggled my hips, trying to take him. He held himself still as I squirmed, as I breathed through the feel of it, of him bottoming out in me. How could he not? His cock was so, so big. But I felt his balls rest against my bottom and I knew I'd taken him.

"Shh," he crooned. "That's it. No pain?"

I forgot all about the fact I was supposed to feel torn open. I'd heard from girlfriends that it hurt. A lot. Like bring ripped in half.

I'd felt pain, at first, but like the sting on my ass that sharp sting evolved, spreading through my veins until every inch of me was on fire. For him.

"More." I clenched down on him and he hissed.

"Lexi, do that again and I'll come before I even start moving."

I had that much power over him? When I did it again, he said some curse words I'd never heard before, his veins bulging from his temples, strain evident on his face.

Clearly, the answer seemed to be yes.

"Then move," I whispered. "Fuck me. I want you to move. I want to feel you slide in and out of me. I want to feel like you're mine."

"Are you sure?" he asked, seeking assurance. I remembered he'd vowed never to hurt me and in this moment, I understood. He'd expected me to have some pain the first time and he had worried that while he was taking his pleasure, he'd be hurting me.

"Yes, mate. I want you. I need you to move."

He pulled back just a bit, then slid back in. Testing.

My eyes fell closed at the feel of his cock sliding over sensitive tissues. I lifted my legs and wrapped them around his hips, locking him to me like a greedy bitch. "Yes, like that."

He pulled back more this time, slid deep. I rolled my hips, rubbing my clit against his body as he rocked into me. God. Yes. This was what I'd been waiting my entire life to experience. I held nothing back. Von was mine and I felt safe in his arms, safe letting go.

"Again. Again. Von. God, please. Don't stop," I said, this time grabbing his back, sliding my hands south and tugging on his ass.

I lifted my hips into his strokes, into the pleasure, and I met him with each thrust, our bodies slapping together. I felt my wetness easing his way, coating my inner thighs.

My clit was hyper sensitive from his mouth, and every time he filled me, he rubbed against it, sparking my need from a banked fire to an inferno. I needed to come again, but this time, I wanted him with me, filling me with his seed, making me his forever.

He moved slowly at first, his thrusts a steady rhythm that made me mewl and whimper and claw at his back. His cadence broke for just a moment, then picked up with even more fervor. In the past, I would lose control, come all over his mouth or his hand while he'd kept his head. It was time for me to watch him lose control, to give in to pleasure, to what my body could make him feel.

"You're mine, Von. You're mine forever."

An unintelligible grunt was his only reply, but when I put my hand on his mark, he reared up. His eyes met mine and he shouted my name. His own hand went to my mark and the circle was complete. Something clicked inside me, like a puzzle piece falling into place, but that piece was Von and for the first time in my life I felt complete.

For a few seconds, I shared his mind as I had in the dream, flooded with his desire, his admiration for me...his love. God, his emotions were so strong I drowned in them, never having dared to hope someone could love me the way he did.

"I love you." I chanted the words as he filled me, unable to contain the emotions flooding my system. Even more astonishing, I realized they were true. He'd cared for me and ensured my pleasure. Honored me, protected me, and desired me every moment we'd spent together. And I'd witnessed his selflessness in battle, his fierce pride and deadly skill, a skill he used to protect those weaker than himself.

As his huge cock filled me, I welcomed him and the bond that would seal us together forever. I gave him everything, heart and soul, mind and body. I held nothing back.

"Lexi." He dropped down over me, his hips slowing to a sensual glide as he looked at me. "I love you, mate. I don't deserve you, but I love you and I'll never let you go."

"Try leaving me and we'll see who gets the next spanking."

The haunted look left his eyes, replaced by mischief as he

lowered his head and kissed me. Our hands entwined, he lifted them over my head and held me still as he took his sweet time sliding in and out of my body, as if he had all the time in the world.

Me, I was more of the dessert first kind of girl, and my body shook beneath his, riding the razor's edge as his tongue filled my mouth, fucking me as his cock fucked my pussy.

When I begged, he finally gave over to the basest of male desires, fucking me like a wildman, his control gone. With one, two more deep thrusts, he came. The feel of his hot seed pulsing inside me pushed me over and I came with him. It was perfection, sublime heat.

While the dream sharing had been intimate, those moments were nothing to this. I'd never felt this close to someone. We were connected. Bonded. One.

There was no going back. And when he slumped down so his head was on the pillow beside me, his weight heavy but comfortingly so, his cock still deep inside me, I knew I never wanted to go back to the way things were before. My place was here on Everis. With the one male in the entire universe that was mine. Von.

"Mate," he murmured. "Mine."

Yes, *mine.*

He was mine.

EPILOGUE

Lexi

"I DO NOT KNOW WHAT YOU ARE MAKING, BUT IT SMELLS wonderful."

"I promised the girls meatloaf and gravy." I'd made friends after Von took me to his home fortress. It was a community surrounded by smaller villages, all of them teaming with everyday people living everyday lives. I was one of the few women who lived in the fortress, but I didn't lack for friends. Besides the other Interstellar Brides, we'd created quite a community with the local women, children.

"Hmmm." He nuzzled my ear, distracting me from the vegetables I was chopping for dinner. "And where is my princess?"

"She's outside feeding Bryn the cookies she sneaked off the counter." Our daughter had just turned three, and she had her daddy wrapped around her little finger so tightly I teased him every time she crawled into his lap demanding an extra bedtime story or extra hugs and kisses.

I thought her at her limit when she'd begged for a pet, but three days later he'd returned from a Coalition mission with a strange little puffball that looked like a cross between a pit bull puppy and a fox. She'd promptly named the beast Bryn, which caused much laughter at dinner that night as she fed the creature treats from her plate beneath the table.

Fuzzy Bryn grew into a beast nearly half my size, yet he never left her side, more a babysitter than pet, and I realized that even in this, Von was loving us, protecting us.

And me? I'd arrived, taken one bite of their horrible food, and promptly taken over the kitchens. Now I had several others working with me to keep the hungry Hunters and their mates well fed. Within a few weeks, I'd completely remade their kitchens and learned Von's favorite Everin meals and shared some of my own from Earth. It had been so much fun to combine both cultures to create exquisite culinary masterpieces. The spices on Everis were exotic and wonderful, but if I, or one of the other brides, craved cinnamon or chocolate from home, Von would order it for me.

Cinnamon delivered via transport across deep space.

Life couldn't get any stranger, but I loved it. Loved every minute I spent with my mate.

Von wrapped his arms around my waist and snuggled up behind me as I stood at the kitchen counter. I felt every inch of him pressed into my back, even the thick ridge of his cock and I leaned into his embrace. "I missed you."

He'd been gone less than two days, but when the Hunters went out on patrol, I always worried. He was mine. Worry went with the territory.

"Daddy!"

"Your daughter did, too," I added.

I turned in his arms to look at both my mate and our daughter. She'd been conceived that very first time. Von hadn't been surprised, considering how many times he fucked me that night. He also didn't doubt his virility, nor my fertility.

I'd heard it only took one time from sex-ed in high school and the woman had been right. To say Von had been thrilled was an understatement. To say that he'd become protective to almost a smothering level was also an understatement. I'd had to endure his constant attentions, love and possessiveness for nine long months.

But when she was born, he transferred the bulk of his protectiveness to her. I wasn't neglected, of course, but Von had been expecting a boy.

A boy to teach to fight, to Hunt, to protect the females of Everis. Instead, out came a dark-haired little girl and he was ruined. Destroyed by love.

A year later, our little one fell in love with her daddy. Two years later, they were inseparable. I had my time with her, but she was definitely a daddy's girl.

I was, too.

Von's eyes were dark with love as he lowered his head and kissed me. The gentle hello quickly became hot and urgent…until little hands tugged at mommy's leg.

"Hungry, Mommy."

I smiled as Von bent to lift her in his arms. When he straightened, emotion swamped me. I wanted another child. A boy, knowing Von's heart would burst with joy at the news.

I wanted a Hunter growing inside me, a strong little boy I couldn't wait to meet. Right here, my entire life was within the circle of my arms, my reason for being.

"Both of you can have a snack before our guests arrive." I grabbed a *breet*, a Everian vegetable that looked quite a bit like a carrot. It was big enough to satisfy her until dinner. She happily took it and quickly began munching, her head dropping to rest in the crook of her daddy's shoulder.

"You spoil her," Von said, but he stroked her long dark hair with undisguised gentleness.

"With a vegetable?" I countered.

"You spoil me, too," he insisted and I couldn't argue. I'd found my bliss on this alien world and I did everything I could to make sure Von knew how I felt.

He grunted and gave our daughter a little squeeze. She giggled around the top of the *breet* but held on even tighter, her small arm like a vise around his neck.

"Just you wait," I added. "Until she grows up and the young Hunters start eyeing her."

His grunt switched to a deep, full-bodied growl. "That will never happen."

"I guess you'd better tell the doctor to get back to work on his stopper formula." My father used to tease me when I was small, threatening to give me the magical *stopper formula* so I would stay little forever. I was teasing Von, of course. I loved teasing him about, well, everything.

"No one will dare speak to her. Cosmo was reassigned to the prison moon, relaying cargo. That punishment will pale in comparison to any male who wishes to mate my daughter. They'll be dead and their body floating across the second galaxy of Naron."

I had no idea where the second galaxy of Naron was, or if it was even real, but I laughed because I had a feeling it was very, very real, and very far away.

"Then don't you think she should have a brother to protect her along with her father?"

Von's eyes flared with instant heat. The attraction never diminished between us. I wanted him more than ever.

"Brilliant thinking, mate." He set our daughter down, who ran gleefully back out to play with Bryn. Once she was well out of hearing range, he turned his heated gaze back to me. "After this dinner, we'll work on your plan. I want you naked, on your hands and knees, ass in the air."

God, I was already wet and we had four more hours of dinner guests and small talk to survive before I could get my mate naked and thrusting inside me. "You do realize you need to come in my pussy to make a baby."

"Is that why it hasn't happened?" he asked, a smile turning up the corner of his mouth. "I guess I will have to stop fucking that tight ass of yours until the job is done."

I didn't like the idea that much and I realized he was teasing me in turn.

"Are you wearing panties now?" he asked, eyeing me carefully.

"Do I ever?" I countered.

"Just checking." A knock at the door turned our attentions and I heard a number of voices outside. Our guests had arrived. Von kissed me quickly, our lips lingering, both of us reluctant to part. "Later, mate. Later."

He went to the door to greet our guests.

Later.

Later there would be tender touches and hot kisses. Laughter and teasing. Wild fucking and slow, gentle rides.

I smiled and rested my palm over my still flat abdomen where our son grew safe and protected, loved. The doctor had confirmed it this afternoon. I would tell Von tonight.

Later, our son would be born, our daughter would grow, and that monster of a pet would protect them both.

Later, Von would bend me over our bed and fill me up,

make me whimper and beg and chant his name. Later, later, later…

Oh, yes. A forever of *laters* sounded absolutely perfect.

————

Ready for more? Read Claiming His Virgin next!

Elite Hunter Zee is scarred from his time in the Hive war leaving him too much of a monster to seduce a beautiful, innocent virgin. Even if his Mark calls to hers, connecting them body and soul, he knows that after just one look at him and she will never surrender the three sacred virginities. Never accept him as a mate.

Blindfolded and seduced, Helen has never seen the Hunter whose voice makes her tremble. She knows something isn't right, but she can't say no to the mysterious and demanding Hunter whose kiss makes her burn, and whose touch makes her beg in the darkness of night.

Zee has everything he thinks he needs, until another takes advantage of his new mate's innocence… and tries to claim Zee's Interstellar Bride for his own.

Click here to get Claiming His Virgin now!

A SPECIAL THANK YOU TO MY READERS...

Want more? I've got **hidden** bonus content on my web
site *exclusively* for those on my mailing list.

If you are already on my email list, you don't need to do a thing!
Simply scroll to the bottom of my newsletter emails and click on
the **super-secret** link.

Not a member? What are you waiting for? In addition to ALL of my
bonus content (great new stuff will be added regularly) you will be
the first to hear about my newest release the second it hits the stores
—AND you will get a free book as a special welcome gift.

Sign up now! http://freescifiromance.com

FIND YOUR INTERSTELLAR MATCH!

YOUR mate is out there. Take the test today and discover your perfect match. Are you ready for a sexy alien mate (or two)?

VOLUNTEER NOW!

interstellarbridesprogram.com

DO YOU LOVE AUDIOBOOKS?

Grace Goodwin's books are now available as
audiobooks...everywhere.

LET'S TALK SPOILER ROOM!

Interested in joining my **Sci-Fi Squad**? Meet new like-minded sci-fi romance fanatics and chat with Grace! Get excerpts, cover reveals and sneak peeks before anyone else. Be part of a private Facebook group that shares pictures and fun news! Join here:

https://www.facebook.com/groups/scifisquad/

***

Want to talk about Grace Goodwin books with others? Join the **SPOILER ROOM** and spoil away! Your GG BFFs are waiting! (And so is Grace)

Join here:

https://www.facebook.com/groups/ggspoilerroom/

GET A FREE BOOK!

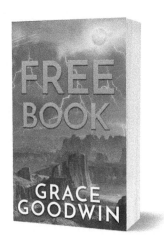

ALSO BY GRACE GOODWIN

Cyborg Seduction

Her Cyborg Beast

Cyborg Fever

Rogue Cyborg

Cyborg's Secret Baby

Her Cyborg Warriors

Interstellar Brides® Program: The Virgins

The Alien's Mate

His Virgin Mate

Claiming His Virgin

His Virgin Bride

His Virgin Princess

Interstellar Brides® Program: Ascension Saga

Ascension Saga, book 1

Ascension Saga, book 2

Ascension Saga, book 3

Trinity: Ascension Saga - Volume 1

Ascension Saga, book 4

Ascension Saga, book 5

Ascension Saga, book 6

Faith: Ascension Saga - Volume 2

Ascension Saga, book 7

Ascension Saga, book 8

Ascension Saga, book 9

Destiny: Ascension Saga - Volume 3

Other Books

Their Conquered Bride

Wild Wolf Claiming: A Howl's Romance

ABOUT GRACE

Grace Goodwin is a USA Today and international bestselling author of Sci-Fi and Paranormal romance with more than one million books sold. Grace's titles are available worldwide in multiple languages in ebook, print and audio formats. Two best friends, one left-brained, the other right-brained, make up the award-winning writing duo that is Grace Goodwin.

They are both mothers, escape room enthusiasts, avid readers and intrepid defenders of their preferred beverages. (There may or may not be an ongoing tea vs. coffee war occurring during their daily communications.) Grace loves to hear from readers!

All of Grace's books can be read as sexy, stand-alone adventures. But be careful, she likes her heroes hot and her love scenes hotter. You have been warned...

www.gracegoodwin.com
gracegoodwinauthor@gmail.com

Lightning Source UK Ltd.
Milton Keynes UK
UKHW021836210221
379147UK00005B/667

9 781795 901710